AF413432

DOE

DOE

REBECCA BARROW

Nancy Paulsen Books

NANCY PAULSEN BOOKS
An imprint of Penguin Random House LLC
1745 Broadway, New York, NY 10019
penguinrandomhouse.com

Edited by Stacey Barney | Design by Kathryn Li | Text set in ITC Gamma

Library of Congress Cataloging-in-Publication Data
Names: Barrow, Rebecca author | Title: Doe / Rebecca Barrow.
Description: New York, NY: Nancy Paulsen Books, [2026] | Summary: High school junior
and cheer team captain Maris becomes locked in a bitter rivalry with a new golden girl,
so when an ancient supernatural creature resembling a doe comes to her in a dream
for help, Maris agrees, only to discover the deal could cost her everything.
Identifiers: LCCN 2026001028 (print) | LCCN 2026001029 (ebook) |
ISBN 9798217006335 hardcover | ISBN 9798217006342 ebook
Subjects: CYAC: Novels in verse | Monsters—Fiction | Supernatural—Fiction |
Cheerleading—Fiction | Family problems—Fiction |
LCGFT: Novels in verse | Paranormal fiction
Classification: LCC PZ5.B28 Do 2026 (print) | LCC PZ5.B28 (ebook)
LC record available at https://lccn.loc.gov/2026001028
LC ebook record available at https://lccn.loc.gov/2026001029

First published in the United States of America by Nancy Paulsen Books, 2026

Manufactured in the United States of America
BVG

ISBN 9798217006335
1st Printing

The authorized representative in the EU for product safety and compliance is
Penguin Random House Ireland, Morrison Chambers, 32 Nassau Street,
Dublin D02 YH68, Ireland, https://eu-contact.penguin.ie.

DOE

1
TEAM

We love the sound of cheer.
Palms slapping thighs, bodies hitting the mat, bones
creaking snapping clicking.
We will be old before our time, maybe, but
that is the future, a time we don't
worry about. Not when
we have circuits to run today and
pyramids to perfect tomorrow and
choreo to memorize yesterday.
Drill it drill it drill it Coach yells.
She's not afraid to cut girls. No weakness, she tells us in her office
after practices, before games.
No weakness. Physically.
Mentally? We're hanging on for dear fucking life,
most of us girls are hanging on by our acrylics.
Coach knows. That's why she gives us
what we need.
Rules and rhythms, running laps
until we sweat, launching back somersaults
straight from standing,
twisting a full three-sixty as we soar through the air,
repeating and repeating
until we can't breathe.
We are not those shiny girls from TV
we have no trophies no medals no rings
we don't compete. Don't have the funds.
Don't have a school that cares, respects us.
We're here because
the pressure does something to
our nerves
something painful and warm.

We're here because
what better way to hurt yourself
than in the pursuit of perfection?

⤙⟶⤚

After practice, sweaty, worn thin,
we run more.
Out of the locker room and to the arms of
people who will pretend they love us
for long enough.
Home to whoever's there, to
the parking lot behind the drive-thru, back seat,
bedroom floor with your best friend,
the one who slept with your ex and lied
but you forgave her because what does it matter when
none of you matter?

2

MARIS

Nell's waiting on the hood of Maris's car.

Waiting for Maris after practice
is the kind of thing girlfriends do
but they are not that, won't ever be,
because Nell is Going Places and Maris
is going to die in this town.

"Hey," Nell calls out to Maris in that
long, languorous way she has, like she's
three tequilas deep
on a hundred-degree day,
but that's just Nell.
Nell, olive skin, sleek dark hair, feline eyes
always watching.
Nell in short skirt, bare legs, no goose bumps
even though it's October and already cold enough to freeze.

"There's some trash on my car,"
Maris calls back, and Nell laughs her
dirty smoker laugh although she's never touched a cig.

Maris walks over, gym bag smacking her splits-sore hip,
waits for Nell to slide down but she doesn't.
"What took you so long?" Nell says. "Everyone else
left ages ago."

What took so long?
Maris replays Coach's voice
snaking into the locker room: *"Larsen,
my office."*

Picking at her already bloody cuticles
as she sat across from Coach
with her perfect pink manicure
and listened to her say
"These goddamn grades, Maris.
How many times do I have to say it?
Do you even want to make it to
senior year? Graduate?"

Of course I do.
I want to graduate.
I want to get a job
and an apartment
and live on my own
so the only shit I have to deal with
is mine.

She looks at apartments
when she is bored in class
or in the middle of the night
sleepless and fantasizing.
Has saved
a list
of places with high ceilings
and beautiful golden light
and shiny wooden floors
arranged in pristine patterns.

Manhattan, mostly,
but she doesn't want to
limit herself
too much. So lately she has widened the search:

Paris
Rome
Barcelona.

She could get a job
one with a fancy title
and a company credit card
and she could live in her pretty apartment
with the golden light
and a doorman who tipped his hat to her
every single day.

Maybe she could. Maybe
some version of her
could.

Out loud she says, "I'll try harder,"
because Coach looks disappointed
and Maris hates letting her down.
Coach is not warm
or sweet
or any of those things,
but she is the only person in Maris's life
who cares about her getting out of West Eaton High.

Closer to a mother
than her actual mom.

⊰⊱

Coach leans back in her chair
and stares at Maris. Her eyes are
dark, like her long hair, stark against her
pale white skin

not a hint of old teenage acne scarring in sight. "You know,
I gave you captain because you worked
your ass off for it.
You're only a junior. It should have been
Kate or Claire,
really." She shrugs. "It was *going* to be
Kate or Claire
but then you showed me how much you
wanted it.
You showed me how much you cared.
You showed me how much you could
focus.
All you have to do
is take that focus out of the gym
and into the classroom."
Coach raises an eyebrow.
"It shouldn't be this hard."

Maris stands, shoving
the chair she was sitting in away,
legs scraping loudly. "I got it,"
she says,
a heartbeat away from a snarl
but she would never snarl at Coach
unless she wanted to spend all of next practice
running sprints by herself.
"I hear you."

Coach calls to her before she steps out of the door.
"It wasn't just the focus," Coach says.
"You're a leader. The team—they never looked at
Kate or Claire
the way they look at you.

So lead them, Maris. Be better.
Or do you want them to follow in your footsteps
so you can all fail out together?"

⊰⊹⊱

"Captain duties"
is what Maris tells Nell now,
and she knows Nell will believe it
because she doesn't care enough to question it.

"Come," Nell beckons, and Maris does
she always does.

Nell kisses Maris, warm mouth, and Maris wishes
like she does too often
that Nell could be a piece of shit just like her.
Then it wouldn't feel so bad
that Nell refuses to love her back.
Won't let Maris
drag her down.

"You need a ride?" Maris asks, and Nell
shakes her head.
"Tutoring," she says.
Yeah, Nell tutors, and Maris
can't get above a D in math.
"You want to come?"
Maris frowns at her. "What,
come sit by you
while you teach some kid geometry?"
"Yeah," Nell says, grinning. "Who knows,
maybe you'd even learn something."

Maris stills, her face
suddenly hot.
Oh, so now Nell
thinks she needs *help?*

For a horrible second
she imagines Nell in Coach's office
Coach shaking her head
and Nell saying *of course, I understand, I'll
try my best with her, but
you know what she's like.*

"I don't need a tutor," Maris says, her words
clipped.
"I need a—"
She is about to say *girlfriend*
remembers it is forbidden
instead says, "A fucking break."

"Fine, don't come!" Nell says, and then her hands
are reaching for Maris, fingers nipping
at Maris's waist.
"But I still have a little time first."

A little time is all it takes
Maris in the passenger seat laid flat
and Nell's mouth working on her
making her forget all about
bad grades
and tutors
and words she can't say.

"Call me later," Nell says
when she's done, a pleased smile

on her beautiful face
and she leaves Maris lying there
still catching her breath.

Nell is always the one who leaves.

3

TEAM

You can't make money in town, not
real money, not enough money
for shitty cars and too-tight dresses and
cigarettes and weed.

So we go a couple towns over
to their glass box mall.
We put on nice-girl dresses, heels
low enough to walk in, hair
scraped back, tied up in silk ribbons.
We sell perfume and lipstick and jewels,
bags and espadrilles and tiny bikinis.
Our customers tip us around Christmas and spring break,
feel bad for us not flying to Mexico or
Palm Springs or
Miami.
Our managers call us good girls, like our gloss,
our appropriate necklines.

It's only after our shifts are done that we
strip.
Back to basics, back to our bones,
hair undone and lips slicked red and feet in battered sneakers,
cutoffs showing so much leg, bras visible through thin tank tops.
Everybody thinks girls like us want to
glow up, grow up.
Why?
We know who we are, what we're made of.
Don't want anything different. We're good at acting,
but when we are in the gym, when we are on the sidelines,
when our bodies are screaming

that's no act.
That's everything we are.

<-<->->

We speed.
We go too fast because how else
can you move,
in a place like this,
a world like this,
where girls like us,
if we stop and stay and stand still,
get told we were asking for whatever shit happened to us.

So we keep moving, always
in the gym
on the roads
only stop when we are safe.
In each other's cars, beds, hearts.

Tonight it's quiet out,
a Thursday, slow night in town,
before the Friday release
the Saturday flight.

What Friday means to us:
practice, short and intense,
that will leave us crawling on the mats.
Then home, to change
tease our hair, tie it up in high high ponies
finger-comb through curls
paint our lips red, pink, coral, plum
and slip into our uniforms,
always a little too tight,
a belt that says *I'm alive.*

But tonight, we drive.
October air crisp
through open windows
the road unspooling before us
like it could go on forever
like we could drive and drive
music up and bodies humming
the horizon always on its way
never quite finding us.

In reality it always ends
and we leave each other
on the doorsteps of apartment buildings, houses
that lean, townhomes
dead on the inside.
We brush our teeth, wipe off our makeup,
change our tampons,
get ourselves off,
text our exes
and go to sleep.
One more day.

One more day. That's it.

⊰⊱

On the way home we see a dead deer on the side of the road.
Swear to god those carcasses are
permanent fixture here,
decaying flesh left
to spoil in the sun.

This one's missing its head.

4
DOE

The creature runs alongside
keeping pace with the car
the one with the girls inside

a shadow matching turn for turn,
mile for mile
although it knows it shouldn't push itself this way
that its body
is no longer built for such
exertion.

Once upon a time it was
pure power.
The familiar shape of a deer, but outstripping
any other of its kind, grotesque and statuesque
a beast that towered above its prey, that if seen
could send humans fleeing in fear, strike terror
into the marrow—

Well. It could have, if
it could have been seen by all humans
but it could—can—only be seen by a select few. Those
who have the same blood in their veins
that was once
used to bind the creature, bind
its power.

Without those binds
it can only imagine the delicious screams it would coax
from the humans.
At its sheer size, mass,

dark velvet flesh and
crown of antlers
looped with the silk of spiders
home for the creatures that roam
the deer's flesh, slip
in and out of pockets of
rot.

Bound, though, it remains in a space
between worlds—roaming the earth, this
earth, but invisible to all the humans it sees.
Correction: not to *all*. There is one—one precious, so
special, so adored.
One who those girls in the car worship
one who has that blood in her veins
that connects her to the creature.
A tie, delicate but tough
diamond bright.
One for whom the deer has
big plans.

But not now, not yet—

For now it just chases, invisible
to the girls in the car
waiting for the time to come
waiting to take
what it wants.

5
TEAM

Do any of us even listen in class?
English to Spanish to World Civ to social studies.
Lunch at the back of the cafeteria,
our own world.
Everyone talks about the geography of
the cafeteria, right?
The class system.
And everyone talks about cheerleaders
dumb girls pretty girls hot girls
but most importantly
popular girls.

Not here. We don't know
exactly
what you have to do to be popular here
but it isn't being us.
No one wants the too-intense
emotionally unstable
rage-filled
no-dreams
no-money
no-future
girls.
We don't exist for our classmates with better lives.
We exist for the girls that come here
already exhausted, worn out from being alive.
Kind of kid who
could set alight at the wrong touch
match to gasoline of desire
loneliness

hunger
wrath.

≺←⊱≻

Friday lunch and
we are sitting at our table
and talking
laughing
screaming
obnoxious and we know it
but then
we mute, because
Jodie
is walking toward us,
Jodie
is wearing a tentative smile,
Jodie—

≺←⊱≻

She used to be one of us, but now
we can think of nothing worse
than being like Jodie.

We remember the scene.
Last year
April.
Jodie
sauntering into practice twenty minutes late
eyes red
not bothering to even try to hide the smell of weed
in her hair, on her skin.

"Hold it," Coach said to us

down on the mats, in
plank position.
So we held
while she spun around
and cut Jodie
right there in front of us
while our arms shook
and sweat dripped from the ends of our noses
decorating the mats beneath.

"Clear out your locker,"
Coach said, her voice
icy bright. "Return your uniform to me
tomorrow."

We heard Jodie's
small gasp, her
"What?"

"You made an agreement when you
joined this team. Show up on time,
prepared,
ready to work. Since you clearly cannot abide
by those terms, then
you are no longer a member of this team. So
clear out your locker, and
return your uniform. You no longer have the
privilege
of wearing it."

Us on the ground,
teeth gritted,
just a few more seconds just a few more—

"That's not fair," Jodie said. "You didn't even
give me a chance—"
"Being on the team *was* your chance."
Coach clapped, and we all heard what she said with it:
You are dismissed.

Still we waited
in plank position
while Jodie crashed through the locker room
until we heard the door to the outside
slam shut behind her.

Only then did Coach speak to us again.
"Okay, girls," she said. "Relax now."

⤙⤚

Jodie stands at the end of our table
and raises a hand
and one by one we
turn
away from her, until she is smiling
at our silent backs

and under the table we find each other's hands
lock pinkies
pretending we are not at all
curious
why she came over
after all this time
promising we will never let ourselves
become the next Jodie.

6

TEAM

We have a half hour between end of school and
beginning of Friday practice.
We change, denim and lace switched for Lycra and polyester.
Then we stretch.
On the mats, sitting as close to a split as we can get,
opening muscles in our inner thighs
while we plan our night.
Toes point and flex, air hisses between teeth as our bodies
warm and loosen
and pinch and protest
and remember, slowly, what they're made to do.

Usually Coach comes in at 3:30 exactly
and by the time she's crossed the gym
we are running.

But today she holds her hands up as she walks in,
wearing one of her dozens of matching black sets
Lycra holding tight to her lithe form
and calls out to us to stop.
"Sit down," she says. "I have an announcement."

We slow, stumbling into each other,
little wind-up dolls whose strings have suddenly been
cut.
Stop . . . running?

But it's what Coach says, so we do, eventually.
Find our spaces on the mat and sit cross-legged
and gaze up at her as if she is our savior,

preacher,
angel.

We don't get announcements,
not usually.
What is there to announce?
We practice on schedule.
Cheer football in fall, basketball in spring.
(No one comes to the games.)
Last time she sat us down like this was to tell us
she was getting a lump in her breast removed
and would be out for a few weeks.
Turned out not to be cancer but for a moment we all thought it,
we thought Coach was gonna get so sick,
and we thought
but she's so pretty
and she's only twenty-five
like age or beauty means anything at all.

So there's a ripple whisper as we sit and stare up
at all five feet two inches of her
and she rocks back on her heels
and then she says, "We have a new member joining the team."

⫷⟶

We explode
talking to each other, over
each other
almost forgetting Coach is there.

  "New girl? Right now?"
 "We don't need another new girl—"
          "—never had one in the
          middle of the—"

$\qquad\qquad\qquad$"Who the fuck is she?"
$\qquad\qquad\qquad\qquad$"If some new bitch thinks she can
$\qquad\qquad\qquad\qquad$just walk in here—"
$\quad$"Put a new girl on the team?"
$\qquad$"What are we supposed to—"
$\qquad\qquad\qquad\qquad$"—is she even good?"
$\quad$"Fuck good, is she one of us?"

And Maris
louder than all of us
directing her words at Coach.
"What's her name?"

⤙⤚

"Genevieve Ray." Coach taps her nails on the clipboard at her hip.
"She's transferring. From my hometown. I trained
at the same gym as her. She's good. We'll use her."

Good?
Coach rarely says we are good, unless it's to
an outsider,
unless she is defending us.
In the gym we are mostly sloppy,
tired,
complacent.
So if Coach ever does call you *good*? If Coach says *nice*, if Coach says
Do it like her?
That girl is queen for the week.

So this girl, this Genevieve—
she's about to be our new queen, we guess.

⤙⤚

We have never had a new girl midyear,
no tryout. It's the third week in October already—tryouts happened
back in the first week of school, where we picked up
little freshman Lo and the three other girls
who have all become part of us now.
It doesn't seem
fair.

But if Coach says she's in, then
she's in.

"When's she coming?"
This from Prairie, braid wrapped round her neck.
She's the kind of blond that comes from a box of at-home bleach
and purple shampoo shoplifted from the beauty supply.
"Does she even *want* to be on the team?"

We hold our breath as one. That's the thing, isn't it?
This team is not for fun, not
for a space on your college app.
We want it, we need it, we feed off it.
And this girl, this Genevieve—

does she know that?
Does she know what this team requires?

❖

Coach fixes Prairie with a stare.
"She'll be here Monday. You will welcome her.
Clear?"

The whispers start again but Coach claps her hands

gunshot loud and
we scatter.
"Enough! Spread out. High knees. *Go.*"

⤛⤜

In the locker room we shower
steal looks at each other's bodies.
Kate has long legs, long silky hair, long eyelashes
we sometimes want to pluck out one by one.
Claire barely reaches Kate's shoulder
but she is an hourglass, mesmerizing, her deep brown skin
always shining (she will not tell
what product she uses
no matter how we poke and prod).
August is visible muscle
and seven piercings in each ear, a scar on her left wrist
that she got from a smashed plate
working in her mom's Vietnamese restaurant
and another scar on her thigh
that we know better than to ask about.
Prairie has freckled white skin and a birthmark on her back,
tattoo of a butterfly under her bra. She has the locker
to the right of Maris, August has the locker
to the left. They are our captain's
closest allies, and so they are almost painfully
subject to our scrutiny.
Maybe if we could learn to be more like them
Maris would love us even more
than she already does.
"She's not serious, right?" Prairie says
while we're sliding damp bodies back into our regular clothes.
"This Genevieve bitch, it's some, like, test or something. Right?"

We give her that look, like she is stupid, like we can't
believe she is even one of us when she talks like that.
We would never ask such ridiculous questions,
if we were in her position.
Besides—when has Coach ever relied on tests? She
doesn't need to. She
puts the fear in us just fine without them.

⊰⊱

"Don't worry." Maris stands on the bench, neon-green bra, her
brown skin bearing the last of a summer bronze,
jeans unbuttoned with her soft belly on view.
We are not skinny, this team, most of us. Maybe we could be
if we tried hard enough, tortured ourselves enough, but
we reserve our masochism for other things.
Outside we are
hedonists.
In here we are strong enough to withstand the hit of a girl,
deadweight on your wrists as you lift a teammate in the air,
elbow to the ribs when she falls,
a kick to your chin.
"If Coach says she's good, then she is. And if Coach thinks she
belongs with us, then she does."
Maris tosses her long black hair, more kinks than curls, raises
one eyebrow. "Unless you think Coach is wrong?"

⊰⊱

Prairie can't shake her head quick enough.
Maris looks satisfied, jumps down as she zips her jeans, tugs them
up around the dip of her waist.
"That's what I thought," she says.

We tumble out of the locker room together,
a mess of *goodbyes, I'll miss yous, call mes*—

things we say to each other even though
we won't be parted for long
before we hang out again tonight.

⊰⊹⊱

We don't say what we're all thinking,
even Prairie.
What if Coach is wrong?

BIRTH

1973

Here is how it started—
a ringing shot
and a girl running into the clearing
where the deer was waiting for her to find it.
Newborn, on shaky legs
but even then too big, and power crackling inside it, pushing
against the seams of its night-black skin.

The girl came sprinting
eager for the spoils of her first real kill—
the body of another deer, the one the creature supposed was
its mother, the one
it had come slithering out of.

The girl came, triumphant grin, and then
uncertain, smile faltering, as the creature
appeared from behind the carcass, coat slick and shining
with blood.
Something strange washed over the girl's face, her brown skin
turning pale, and she
swallowed.
Held out a trembling hand
for the creature to approach.

"Hi, little one," the girl said, a whisper. "It's okay, it's okay—"

The creature ventured forward, taking in
the girl—thin, exhausted, a film of grime that looked
impossible to remove.
It flicked its red tongue out to lick
her fingers

tasting the salt of her skin
the earthiness of the dirt on her.
Then it stepped back
looked up at the girl
and blinked.

"Hold on," the girl said. "Wait here, okay?"
The creature mewled in response, instinctual,
its words spoken directly into the girl's mind.

Please, don't be long.

And the girl gasped, threw her hands up
over her ears
and scrambled back. The uncertainty replaced with
fear.

"Hold on," she said again, and then she was
gone.

The creature waited, licking blood
from the carcass beside it. Didn't have to wait long, though,
before the girl came back
in a truck, bed carrying
another handful of girls.

The creature blinked again. It did not know how it knew
all these things—words, sensations, mechanical machines—
but it knew, as surely
as it knew its own
power.

The girls climbed out of the truck
and made their way over to the creature,
keeping a distance. They all looked the same
as the first girl: tired

and on edge
and curious
but afraid.

"What do you mean, it
talked to you?"

They whispered, as if
they needed to hide. "I swear," the first girl said. "I was talking
like how you talk
to an animal, and I said *hold on, wait here,*
and it made this little noise like—like—I don't know, a
kitten or something,
but then inside my head I heard
a voice."

The tallest girl ventured forward. She
was the leader, the creature already knew. A grit to her
that the others lacked.

This time when the creature spoke, it didn't bother
to camouflage its words
with an outward sound.
This time it kept its mouth shut
and let the words ring in the girls' heads, no pretense, no
artifice.

Don't be afraid.

A silky whisper into their consciousness, like a snake
slithering
venom hidden.

I won't hurt you.

There came a collective gasp, and then
action.

The carcass loaded into the bed of the truck
the creature scooped up into a sling fashioned
from one of the girls' shirts.
Then driving through the dried-out field
toward a lonely house
where more girls spilled out
and the creature was welcomed
home.

BIND

The girls called it a farm
although the creature saw no animals
and what crops it saw were
withering.

And the house itself—
old and
withering.
But home for these girls
who had nowhere else to go, the creature knew.
Could read it in them, easing into their minds
learning their names
and discovering their deepest secrets:

Samia and the sister she left behind
Dawn and the pain in her ribs, broken and rebroken
Crystal returning to an empty house, family moved on without her
Iris and her dancer dreams crushed
under the weight of her mom's boyfriend
Bonnie and the baby she wasn't even allowed to hold
before it was taken away, her parents
only too eager to have their good girl returned, as if she could
put it all behind her
easy.

All of them
and the others
flocking to this place because it promised love
hope
sanctuary.

So the girls brought the creature to that home
and Iris—the leader—was the only one who had the slightest idea
of what they had brought into their midst.

"I've heard about these things,"
the girl said, preaching to her followers
as the creature listened.
"Way, way back, stories passed down from my ancestors
before they were brought to this country. They have different
names—gods, monsters, spirits—and people believe
different things about them—that they want to help, or want to
hurt—
and they can live for centuries
but one thing is always the same:
They are powerful beyond
anything you can believe. And if we know what's good for us
we have to bind it."

At those words the creature stood
tottering on unsteady legs
and felt that power rushing in its veins
and opened its mouth, ready to sing, channeling the power
through the threads of song
as its kind always had.

But its voice came out thin, weak, and instead of unleashing—
instead of the power grabbing hold of the girl
and silencing her, tossing her across the room
as punishment
for daring to suggest such a thing—all that happened
was a wind that circled the girl Iris
blowing her hair around her face

and all the girls began to laugh in delight,
cooing at the creature,
and it cursed the frail, brand-new body it was inside of,
too weak to even channel its own power properly.

Too weak to resist the girls
as they planned how to contain it
restrain it.

It begged them
burrowing into their minds to speak:

You're making a mistake—
I can help you better if you leave me unbound—
I promise to never hurt you—

But Iris made the decisions
and Iris lowered herself to the creature's level
eye to eye.
"You say that now
but who knows what would happen in the future?
We have to protect ourselves. We have to
protect you, too.
You don't know the world you're in
or the people out there
what they think about anything outside the norm—
anything they can't explain.
If they saw you, they'd kill you."

If you understood me like you say you do
then you wouldn't do this to me.

Iris nodded slowly, her face
full of sorrow.

"You're wrong. It's because I do understand you
that I know we have to do this."

So the creature had no choice
but to sit and watch as the ritual got underway.
As an altar was built
out in the woods
where the girls offered their own sacrifices:
treasured trinkets, knots
of hair, rivulets
of blood,
tied into wreaths with wildflowers snatched from the forest floor.

Under a new moon the girls—
thirteen in total—
circled the creature and passed around
a candle
and a knife.
Pricked their fingers and pressed
bloody prints onto the wax, and held the creature down
so Bonnie could nick its throat
and hold the candle to the blood that came forth.

The creature watched
as Bonnie handed the red-marbled candle to Iris
who lit it, the flicker beneath her chin
casting shadows on her already haunted face.
"Through this ceremony we will be
forever connected, a bond
unbreakable. We vow to honor that bond, to honor
the creature, to protect it
in all its glory."

The creature stared as Iris stepped outside of the circle
and tipped the candle, dripping wax onto moss, drawing
a closed ring around their tangled collection
of souls. "Repeat after me," she said. "We receive this gift—"
"We receive this gift," the girls echoed.

We receive this gift—

The creature said it without meaning to, without
being able to stop. It opened its mouth to mewl again
but that didn't stop it from repeating each line Iris said, in rhythm
with the rest of the girls.

"We receive this gift,
and vow to care for this creature, as we pray it will
care for us.
We recognize its power, but know
that power uncontrolled may damage us
beyond repair. In caring for this creature, we bind its powers
and limit their reach, for the good of us all.
In caring for this creature, we forge a
sacred connection
with the offering of our blood, and the creature's.
No other human but those of us here
who gave our blood to this spell
and our descendants, who will share our blood
and our sacred connection,
will be able to see this creature.
To all other humans
it will be invisible, unseen.
We thank whatever power
created this being
and sent it to us.
With our offerings we give ourselves
and in return may it care
for us, use its powers for good,

for us.
Bless this creature
and bless us all."

The creature felt its eyes widen
in fear
as Iris stepped back inside the circle and stood above
its body.
"Show us," Iris said
quiet, reverent. "Make it
rain." She tipped the candle and poured
molten wax onto its forehead
and the creature cried out in pain.
But not only from the burning—from the sensation of threads
tying tight around its limbs, wrapping
around its ankles, throat, heart.
Invisible but indelible
and as its voice keened
a fat drop of rain kissed its burning forehead.

Suddenly the sky opened
and urgent, cool rain doused the group in the woods, drenched
the gasping ground, the drought that had plagued these woods
and the farm
and the land for miles around
finally abated.

The creature struggled
to its feet
while the girls tipped their faces up to the rain
laughing in delight.
Iris spun, droplets skimming off her skin. "I said
the creature's power could help us,
and look—"

Beneath the earth, where the creature stood,
roots began to awaken.
Leaves unfurling, fruits
beginning to gestate. The creature could feel it happening
deep down below, and it knew
the girls felt it, too.

"With our offerings
we bound its power to nature," Iris said. "Think
of what this creature will be able
to do. Think of what
this means for us."

The rain
washed away blood and dust, the effort
of surviving
eased a little now
by the gift the creature had given them—
or been forced to provide, its true strength trapped
beneath the bindings put upon it.
"We'll be able to grow food again," one girl said.
"The stream will run again," said another.
"Maybe we could grow flowers to sell," said a third.

The creature watched them dance.
                              What have you done to me?

Bonnie crouched in front of it, the only one
willing to stop dancing and pay attention
to what the creature said.
"Here," she said in a quiet voice, almost lost
beneath the noise of the rain, the girls
shouting their joy. She picked up one of the wreaths
and laid it upon the creature's head, then sat back on her heels,

curious, eyes scanning the creature's face. "I know
you're not a deer, not really, but
you look like one. And I think you should have
a name. Are you a boy or a girl?"

The creature looked back at her.

I am all, and I am nothing.

The girl nodded. "Okay," she said, and then even quieter,
if that was possible,
like she was talking only to herself: "My baby, the one they
took away from me—she was
a girl. I didn't get to name her but
she was a girl. But I want to name you, now."
She looked over to Iris, their leader, and
leaned in closer. "I think we'll just call you
Doe."

7

TEAM

Sky above is bruise black
and we swing from rusted metal frames,
bellies full of vodka-spiked slushies and
gas station delicacies.

"Here." August holds her phone up, triumphant. "Found her."
Come on.
You don't give a group of girls like us a full name
and not expect us to discover every part of their online existence.

She's not bright, this Genevieve Ray,
at least not enough to have all her shit set to
private.
We crowd each other, pulling up profiles on our own phones,
clicking tags,
scrolling

        scrolling

            scrolling.

⫷⫸

We stare at the screen.
Genevieve Ray,
artificial blonde
(an inch of roots, ashy brown),
bronzed skin
(from a bottle or real? is she white? Latina? just
light-skinned? can't tell),
neat nails.
Pretty round face with a ski-slope nose
carefully sculpted brows above dark eyes
vicious smile.

⊰⊹⊱

There she is, top of the podium.
There she is, arm around another girl
another girl
a boy
an older woman
two more girls.

There she is
arm around Coach,
our Coach,
except this girl doesn't even call her Coach, right?
Genevieve probably calls her by her name, like
friends, like
sisters.

⊰⊹⊱

"Look at the medals," Claire says, flicking her long braids,
this month a sweet mix of jet-black and iridescent pink shimmer,
over her shoulder.
"If she's so good, why is she switching to cheer?"

"Why is she coming here at all?"
August shakes her head, soft cropped waves sweeping her ears,
and then reaches to scratch at the shaven nape of her neck.
"We had to
work to make this team. Be part of it. And what,
this girl gets to just walk in?"

"I bet she's afraid."
This from Lo, perched
on the bottom of the slide
arms wrapped around herself

39

in a too-big denim jacket
Bambi eyes blinking. "I mean,
I was afraid, at tryouts, and when I found out
I made the team. Maybe she feels
the same."

Prairie wrinkles her nose.
"That's
not the same.
You and her
are not the same."

"I know," Lo says
hands fluttering around her face now
cheeks pinkening. "I just mean,
like, if she's afraid, maybe we could be
like, welcoming, or something?"

"You want to head up the committee?"
August snaps at Lo now. "Oh, let's get
streamers! And a banner! Is that what
you'd like?"

We watch Lo shrink, hear the
sting
of August's words landing. "No,"
Lo says, even quieter
than she usually is. "I just—
I'm stupid. Forget it."

⤜⬩⤛

Maris kicks off the swing set.
"Look. I said it earlier.

If Coach says she's right,
then I'm on board. And if she's not right—"
Maris smiles.
"We'll find out soon enough."
And she has that look in her eye
the one we all love
the one everyone else fears.
The look that means
Maris is going to strip you piece by piece until you are
nothing.

If Maris is right, and Coach is right,
then this Genevieve,
she'll survive.
It'll make her stronger.
If she can't take it?

She'll be glad for the chance to get out
while she can.

8
GENEVIEVE

Her first Friday night in this town
and Genevieve's breath comes hard
as she sprints up the hill.

First day of school on Monday
first practice afterward.
She has to be
prepared.

The warning rings in her ears
as she crests
and stops, hands on her head
sweat sticking her clothes to her skin.

I told the team all about you.
They're looking forward to meeting you.
They're good, but
a little rough around the edges. I think you being there
will show them how much
better
they could all be.
So don't be afraid to show off.
And don't be afraid
if they try to push you a little. You can handle it.
I'll see you on Monday.

Genevieve turns to gaze
down the hill, her new town
laid out and lit up before her.
They're only here because her dad
lost his last job—budget cuts

at the university—and the only new job he could find
was at an old college friend's company
selling furniture.
Had to leave their house, their town,
all Genevieve's friends
all her memories
and come here, a place
that seems halfway dead.

Her mom is always worried
about her running in the dark, but Genevieve
feels no fear.
She runs down the hill
and turns, prepares for her next sprint
back up.

GROWTH

The creature grew,
impossibly fast,
like the crops that bloomed in abundance now
thanks to her power.

The bindings still
chafed
but as the creature grew
she found the ties seemed to grow with her
felt a little
looser, a little
less like a prison
and more like the protection the girls promised.

The creature grew,
impossibly large,
strong and muscular, coat
glossy and warm. A set of
arcing antlers appeared, and the girls
adorned them
with flowers picked from their thriving garden,
bells and beads they found at the market.

They grew together: the girls
getting stronger, sleeping better, no longer
surviving but
living. The farm became
bountiful and rich, guided by
the creature and her nature-bound power, bringing
rain to nourish the ground,

sun to unfurl leaves,
frost to cover sleeping perennials.

Yes, the creature itched at the boundaries of its power,
sometimes.
Closed her eyes at night and saw visions
of the beast she could have been
the terror she was meant to leave in her wake
but even bound
she could still shock and surprise. Found herself
wanting to please the girls further
deciding to conjure
sudden snowfall, pillowy drifts for the girls to play in,
where they returned to
children, acting out the childhood most of them
never really experienced.
The creature sang her songs—
stronger now, vibrant melodies
inhuman but beautiful—and drew rainbows
across the sky, lit up
comets, brought
rolling thunder and crackling lightning
when she needed release. But she found release, too, in
fulfilling every request the girls made
choosing the right notes
to deliver what they needed.
And she grew to love
watching the girls gorge on the fruits of her creation—
mouths dripping red with the juice of plump strawberries, hands
bloody from butchering
the cows they now earned enough money to keep,
gnawing flesh from bone
charred on a hot grill.

She learned the distinct voice of each girl—
Bonnie's soprano laugh and
Iris's quietly sparkling voice, and
how Luella chattered as she wove ribbons through the creature's
antlers, and how the name *Doe* sounded out of each girl's mouth.
The name she accepted—first reluctantly, and then
gladly—knowing that
this was her home, that these girls
were her family.

And Doe understood
why they had felt the need to protect her:
how the residents of the nearby town
talked of the girls
whispering under their breath
cult
mothers gathering their daughters close
and keeping them away from those strange and unusual girls
freaks and *runaways* and *twisted*.

But it was okay
at the farm
away from the rest of the world, who could never
understand.
At home they were safe
and the creature was adored,
worshipped.
Nothing could hurt them.

◄◄►►

That was the way things went,
peaceful and fine.

Until—

One day the girl Bonnie came home from the market
alone
and stumbled out of the truck
into the grass
where she fell and lay for a while
calling out for help.

Doe heard her call first
the others out in the fields harvesting
too far away.

She left the half-built shed
which the girls had made into her home
and trotted around the side of the house
finding Bonnie there, prone.

Bonnie?
Bonnie, wake up—

Doe nudged her, nuzzling her nose against Bonnie's shoulder
and the girl's eyes opened wide
and the creature noticed:
the blackened soles of her bare feet
the torn dress
the smeared shadows around her eyes
and—

the smell,
sour
rancid
hot.

Doe's nostrils widened, lips
pulling back over her teeth

and her words in Bonnie's mind were
urgent, full of
fear:

> *Tell me what happened.*

Bonnie blinked, her hands
curling into the grass. She sat up
slowly, mouth opening
closing
opening again.
"Oh, Doe," she said, a sob
lodged in her throat. "He—
he caught me. I couldn't
get away."

She didn't have to say anything more.
Doe understood
and all at once she became hot, flesh
burning with rage.

She ran into the fields
to collect the others, to tell them
what had been done to Bonnie
and the girls sprinted back, Iris
leading them.

It did not take long for them to coax
the name out of Bonnie's mouth, or the story—how
Lucas Mayweather, the son of one of the town's
oldest families, who sold
honey at the market, came by the stall,
like he always did, and flirted
with Bonnie,
like he always did, but this time

did not like her laughter, the way she
told him no
and so he had grabbed her by the hair
and dragged her from the market into an alley
and nobody had done anything to stop him
nobody had even looked
her way.

Iris put Bonnie to bed
and when she came back, she looked each girl
in the eye, and then at Doe, and said,
"Something must
be done about this."

Doe bent her head
and Iris placed her hand on Doe's nose, her touch
soft and warm.

I have an idea.

9

TEAM

We drink a little more
dance in the sandbox
watch Maris climb the jungle gym
too rickety to be safe
but what is safe?
We are prone to injury
and we wear them
with pride.
Broken bone, bruised flesh,
anything and everything we brandish
like a prize.

◄←►►

On the ground Prairie lays flat on her back
as she stares at her phone.
"Genevieve Ray. Gen-e-vieve,"
she says, syllables stuck on her tongue,
and we all hear it.

Gen, maybe.
She could fit, if she were Gen,
slot into place with the rest of us: Cami and Lo,
Kate, Claire, Vi.
Nicknames we've rolled around our mouths
until the edges are smoothed off,
words we use to display our ownership of each other,
when Maris is sometimes just Mare, when August becomes
only her last name,
Grimes! yelled through crowded hallways.

Maybe we will get to know her inside and out
the way we know each other.
Claire keeps an altar in her room
where she prays for her dad's Parkinson's
to slow down.
Kate can't sleep without reciting the poem her mom wrote
in the card she left before she ran away
the only Arabic she knows.
Little Lo has periods so bad
she sometimes throws up from the pain.
Prairie (three older brothers
and a dad who rules
with fear)
didn't know how to use a tampon
until Maris taught her how.
And August—August has been in love with Maris
since the day they first met.

⊰⊹⊱

"Grimes!"
Maris yells now, ordering August
up there on the jungle gym with her,
and of course August climbs.

We don't always do what Maris tells us to,
just—
most of the time.
Every team has their captain,
their ruler,
and she is ours, a power we are glad to give her.
Of course August always does what she is told
but she can't help
what being in love
does to her.

Once upon a time we thought Maris might
love her that way
too, that maybe
they would lead us together, but then
Nell arrived on the scene, and
we felt stupid, silly, like
a little kid wishing her divorced mommy
would get together with her favorite teacher.
We can only have one leader
and Maris can only want
the other girl.

At the top of the rusted metal structure August howls
and Maris looks at August, so proud.
Another Maris look we love,
when you feel you've done the right bad thing,
when she looks like she could just eat you up.
We know it stings August
but she'll never stop chasing those looks
just like we never will.

"See?"
Maris throws an arm out
to encompass all that is before us,
empty fields and crumbling homes.
"All of this is ours, girls.
Don't you forget that."

REVENGE

The girls wanted revenge.
Doe did, too, but
her powers remained limited,
bound.
She could not
toss the boy around
at the end of an invisible rope
shattering his skull and pulverizing
his organs.
She could not
warp his mind
create a torturous pain in his psyche
to leave him screaming,
begging for mercy.
All of those old
fantastical magical torments
the punishments of fairy tales
ancient myths
that belonged to Doe's true unbound nature
were off-limits. She could not
enact any of the fantasies
fighting in her mind.

Her power now
was connected solely to nature
and up until now Doe had only used that power
for the most obvious means: to help the girls, to grow
crops, and to create
lazy spring-perfect days. But she could bring
storms, too,
and that was how the idea took root.

The streets were quiet
on the night Doe and the girls
took to them.

Running through the quiet
leaving the truck behind, hidden
on a side road where no one
would see it, where they could get back
for a swift escape.

Running
and Doe knew how it must look from the outside—
just a group of girls, wild things
doing whatever their twisted nature told them to. Wasn't that
how everybody around here
thought of them? They wouldn't see
the creature in their midst, couldn't see her mass moving, couldn't
know
what she was about to unleash.

In all honesty
Doe was uncertain, unsure
if her plan would deliver the right results. She had never done
anything like this
before—
but for Bonnie, she would do anything.
For all of these girls, to whom Doe was connected
by blood,
she would do anything within the limits
they had set.

Wind whipped in their wake
as they approached the house on the hill.

Bonnie began to protest—she was
nothing but rage now, the
injustice of what had been done to her
turned into hot fire, and she wanted to see
their revenge take place—
but Iris cautioned her, and led them off, all
thirteen of them,
hiding some distance from Doe, waiting
at the bottom of the hill.

The weather had been calm all day.
Doe made it so, knowing
that a sudden storm
would draw people out of their homes, to
batten down the hatches.

An image of Bonnie lying
shocked in the grass
filled Doe's mind.

Time to
act.

She opened her mouth
unhinged her jaw
and began to sing—

this time the song was sharp, discordant,
a clash of crashing waves and shattering glass

and the sky above began to roil,
dark, heavy.

The wind became a gale
and the house on the hill began to shake, earth
shifting beneath it.

Doe added another thread to the song
and moonlight disappeared behind clouds, the only light instead
the flash of lightning, cracking
across the sky
illuminating the figures fleeing,
stumbling out of the house
as the unnatural storm
reached its crescendo.

There he was.
Doe picked him out immediately:
blond prince, hands over his head, watching
his home tremble.
Monster.

Another note to the song
rising from a bottomless pit somewhere
deep inside,
a song older than Doe herself could even guess at.

The next time the lightning came
it forked through the black night
aimed right at its golden target.

One strike
a second

third
and over, over, over again.

Doe could smell him from where she stood,
the burnt flesh of him,
and a woman screamed
and Doe brought the lightning down again
again
again—

The song slowed. Notes
crawled back into Doe's throat
and when she closed her mouth, when
it was done,
the golden boy was little more
than a smoking husk.
Charred and still, his mother's scream
carrying on the last of the wind.

Doe turned to where the girls hid.

Come, quickly. We can't stay too long.

And they slipped away, keeping low, through
long grass, knowing
no one up on the hill was paying the slightest attention
to anything down there.

By the time they heard sirens
they were on their way home, girls
in the truck, crammed into the bed, Doe
keeping pace alongside them.

Not for the first time

she wished for a way out of her bindings, from the protection
the girls had given her
if only to stare the dead boy in the face
and rip his throat out
with her teeth.

10

MARIS

They are still at the playground
when headlights sweep over them
and Maris feels herself glow.
Nell, behind the steering wheel,
and it's time for Maris to leave.

"Be good," she calls over her shoulder
laughing
as if they have any idea how to do that.

She slips into Nell's car
where it's warm, aux cord playing trip hop,
cherry soda sweating in the cup holder.
"I got you fries, too, but I got hungry,"
Nell says,
and Maris rolls her eyes,
takes a sip of the soda.
"I hate you," she says
to make Nell laugh.

Except Nell doesn't, only
nods toward the outside world.
"No," Nell says, "*she* hates me."
Maris follows her gaze
to August,
out there pretending
she isn't paying any attention
to what's going on in this car.

Maris chews her straw.
It's not like she doesn't know

how August feels about her.
She just pretends not to.
She just pretends not to notice
the face August makes
when she has to say Nell's name, and
the way August always holds her hand during a stunt
a fraction longer, tighter, than is
strictly necessary, and
how she's always so eager to do
exactly what Maris tells her to.
It's easier that way, easier
to ignore
because August is cute, cool, a bitch, sure,
but she doesn't like August like that.
Maybe if Maris were a different person
a different version of herself
she would like August like that
let things be easy and expected.
They could grow up together.
After high school August would
give in
to her mother's wishes
and take over the family restaurant. Maris
could do the books in the back
and tolerate August's mother
sneaking religious paraphernalia into their house.
Maybe they'd have a fucking dog.

She bites clean through the straw.

There is no other version of her
so this is the way things are.
And she has Nell—

(Nell, who looks down on you
even though she comes from the same roots
Nell, who's making something of herself
while you run around
in too-short skirts
that Nell?)

—she has Nell
and she's not about to let
August's jealousy
fuck it up.

"Ignore her," Maris says now
and reaches over
to stroke a finger up Nell's throat
under her chin.
"She doesn't bite."
She leans over.
"But I do."

PUNISHMENT

In the aftermath
Doe was left reeling.
Had not found a way to free herself of the bindings entirely—
was not sure she wanted to, not when that was what connected her
so closely
to the girls—
but she had found a way to get close
to the violent beast she was meant to be.

In the aftermath
Doe saw that the girls were satisfied,
satiated. All those years of
being powerless, their childhoods of
being beaten, screamed at, tossed aside, unable
to fight back—
now they had a weapon, they told her. Now no one
could cross them, not without
punishment.

No one could ever know it was them.
So they and Doe thought, anyway.
How could they be responsible
for a natural disaster? How could they be responsible
for lightning striking that boy dead? For a
freak accident?

And it was true: No one could
prove
it was them
that Doe was the architect
of that death.

But that didn't matter. It was enough
for people in town to know
that those girls out there on that farm . . .
there was something *wrong* there.

And so the girls started coming back from the market
carrying everything they'd taken to sell.
"No one will buy from us," Crystal said. "They won't even
walk by the stand. They think we had something to do
with what happened."
And here she looked at Doe. "They say
we're witches."

> *Of course they do. They don't understand*
> *anyone like us, anything they can't*
> *explain.*

Doe came closer to Crystal
lowered her head to rub
against the girl's cheek.

> *You are the ones who told me that.*
> *See how right you were?*

Doe meant to bolster their spirits, remind them
that they had always known what
people out there
thought of them. She told Iris
not to let fear creep in, and in turn
Iris commanded the girls to keep trying, but
before long
they stopped going to the market at all.
They could live off what they grew, Iris said—
they'd survive.

But soon it was more than
whispered words.

A gun
pointed at Samia as she walked through the woods,
crossing the path of a hunter
his aim fixed on her until she backed away, trembling hands
held high.
Red paint
slashed across their front door, over
the windows, giving everything inside
an otherworldly feel.

Doe paced the same path
back and forth
in the field behind the house. Now she wished
to be fully freed, unbound, so she could
destroy the people targeting the girls for a crime
they didn't even commit.

It's not fair,
she told Bonnie.

After what that boy did to you
he got what he deserved. But now you all
are paying the price for what I did, and I only did it
because of what he did. Even now he's dead
he still brings trouble.

"It's okay," Bonnie said, sounding
tired, laying her head
against Doe's cheek. "Nobody
blames you. You did that for me. I'm so
grateful. And you don't have to worry about
these little attacks. They can't see you. You'll always be safe."

⤛⬩⤜

It was the smoke that woke Doe.

11
MARIS

When Nell drops her home that night
the street is quiet, houses asleep.
Except for theirs,
because Maris can see from here
the flicker of the TV
through the half-closed curtains.

Inside Celia Larsen is on the couch
staring at the TV.
Doesn't mention
how late it is
how Maris smells like booze
how she has another girl's lip gloss
smeared over her chin.
Jesus, no—any of that
would require her mother
to notice anything at all.

"Mom."
Celia looks up at the word
and her eyes focus on Maris
but that doesn't mean she's
seeing her.

"Oh," Celia says. "Hi, sweetie."

Maris bites down
on the inside of her cheek.
Always *sweetie, darling, my love.*
"You should go to bed,"

Maris tells her mother.
"It's late."

"Mmm," Celia says, like she's
agreeing, but all she does is
turn back to the TV
and disappear.

⤝⤞

She hasn't always been this way.
Maris knows that. She tries
to remember
that her mom is sick, that depression
is a sickness
that takes and takes and takes
so it is not that her mom has given up on loving her
it's just that
there's so little left for her to give.

But that's why she has
the team
her girls.
They love her enough
to make up for it. They
adore
her, don't they?
How did Coach put it? Oh yeah: I'm a
leader. They
look to me.
Leader is a nice way to say
Maris won't be told what to do.
Ever since she was a
little girl

she's been that way: They played
her games, the way
she wanted to play.
And now the team does what
she tells them to, because she is their
captain. Fearless leader.

⤙⤚

(Sometimes she does
fear—
that they want too much from her
that they rely on her too much
that she can't possibly give them all they want
can't possibly be the girl they believe her to be
because after all
how can they look up to a girl
who barely has a plan for her own future?
Who can't see further than
graduation?
She knows some of her girls
will leave her. All of them will leave
eventually
and who will Maris be left with?
Not Nell, that's
for sure. She's going to fly
the furthest of them all.)

(So sometimes she does
fear—
that she isn't worth their love and adoration
because after all
even her own mother can't always love her.)

RETRIBUTION

Smoke burrowing into Doe's nostrils, saturating her
skin.
By the time she came to, heaved herself up off the ground and
out of the shed, the fire
was out of control. Flames
licking
the night sky,
eating
through the house.

No. No no no—

Tires squealed
and Doe saw a truck tearing down the road,
away from the house, away from
the scene of the crime.

She ran to the house
calling rain as she moved, Doe
already knowing, somehow, that it was
too late.

Still, she sang, and the rain came
dousing the flames
but it was already over.
The wooden frame of the house smoldering and splintered
but the shiny metal of brand-new padlocks unharmed, locking
the doors, the windows, so there was
no escape.

She picked her way through the house in silence.
No sirens headed their way.
Used her teeth to drag the bodies out onto the damp grass—
what was left of them, anyway.

When she closed her eyes, she could only see
the girls waking to find flames slipping under their doors, burning
hands on hot doorknobs, running
for the exits, only to find themselves
locked in. Trapped.
Banging on the windows, on the walls, calling
for Doe to come help them, for Doe
to save them.

Thirteen bodies, flesh
scorched and oozing, blisters
burst open, mouths
frozen wide in screams.

Iris and Bonnie
curled together, protecting each other
to the last moment.
Doe licked
what remained of Bonnie's hand
and turned in the direction of town.

12

MARIS

Sometimes Maris wishes
her mother could just go all in
and leave.
A physical absence
to match the mental one.

Is she a
bad mother?
Maybe not.
She doesn't hit Maris.
Doesn't abuse her.
She's just—

not Present.

In years past she has been.
There have been times where she could make it
to school meetings or remember to sign
permission slips, remember that Maris
needed new shoes, underwear, glasses.

But all that was a long time ago.
Now she is mostly Gone.

Her dad isn't around,
used to come see her when she was little,
when her mom was still Present,
but then Maris grew up
developed tits and an ass and a foul mouth
started telling the world she was queer, a lesbian, a
dyke (big smile, eyes flashing)

and he didn't know what to do with all that
so now he sends
twenty bucks on her birthday
and promises dinner plans
that always fall through.

It's funny,
Maris always thinks:
Her dad doesn't want to see her
and her mom can't.

If no one sees you
do you even really exist?

⊰⊱

Inside this house I am a ghost.

ISOLATION

As dawn broke
the tornado hit. Spiraled through
sleepy streets, taking down
churches and schools and homes, lifting
cars and tossing them, sucking
dirt and debris up up up
and letting it fall.

Doe sang it into existence, careening through town, leaving
nothing but destruction in her wake, a
message to the guilty.

In the days after
the air still
the town shell-shocked
she walked through the wreckage
and realized how
none of this mattered. All these people
faces tear-streaked
skin gray with exhaustion
sifting through the wreckage
yet, of course, no one
saw Doe as she passed by.

And she realized.
None of this
would bring the girls back.
They were dead,
gone,
and that left Doe—

trapped.
Bound, still, her power—
her existence—
constricted. The words they had recited
and the sacrifices they had offered
had been meant for safety—theirs and
Doe's. But now
the girls were gone to ash, and Doe
remained where she had always been—
bound, to be unseen,
forever.

13
MARIS

In a dream—

Maris walks
barefoot, the ground wet beneath,
tracing the yellow line
through the center
of the road
until she comes to the
crossroads.

There, in the middle of it all,
a black deer stands, powerful,
poised,
like a ballerina en pointe,
like Maris at center position, hip cocked.

She closes her eyes
slow shutter speed,
freezing an image of this rotted creature
as it stands there,
skeletal, flesh
melting away from bone and
spider-silk-strewn antlers
arcing high.

The creature looks back at her
through milky white eyes
curious
and calm.

Maris steps forward,
unthinkingly.
A pull.
From it to her,
a feeling
she knows from the girls,
that feeling of connection
earthed through sad roots
and salt sweat.

"Hello," her dream self says.
"Have you been waiting long?"

14

DOE

Doe moves forward
lowers her head,
and the girl comes to her, places
her cheek against Doe's face.
A move that is so
familiar, so
sweet.

Not long at all.
Come, let's walk. Tell me
all about your day.

The girl smiles and
together they walk
in the middle
of the empty road
off into the darkness.

BEREFT

After Doe
lost her girls
there was nowhere to go
and everywhere.

So she wandered, unseen and
untouched
untethered.

A year, then two
a decade
more, the years
passing at first slow, then
so fast.

Untethered, but still bound
by the spell the girls had cast
so that no human saw her imposing inky mass
or heard her discordant song.
No one to adore,
adorn her.

The world changed around her
and she began to change, too:
rotting
as the decades passed
a breaking down accelerated
without the girls there to care for her
without the will to care for herself.
She saw herself reflected in
silver mirror lakes

and examined herself through eyes turned from crystal
to cloud.

Maggots inching across her haunches,
spider's web strung thick and heavy between antlers, the insect
scuttling across a jaw stripped half to bone
no more blossoms to decorate her crown.
She was invisible to humans
but not to the natural animal world
and at first she hated them
used her
nature-bound powers
to send them running, hiding
but no matter what they returned
and soon Doe came to know them
as part of her.

She rotted
and thought of her girls
left to do just the same
left for the flies and maggots
that surely burrowed beneath their
melted skin.

She dreamed sometimes
of the life she had imagined unfolding
when the girls were still alive.
Thriving
even as her body decayed
what flesh and coat there was left
kept shiny and clean
by the girls' devotion.
Watching the girls become women

growing older beside them
watching them become mothers, perhaps
using her powers to make flowers bloom
for a new generation.

Or maybe her girls
would eventually have given her the mercy
of death.
Looked at her rotting form and
unbound her
let her powers run free
for a sweet, blissful moment
and then ended her life
returned her to the mystical plane
from which she first came.

But those were only dreams.

Doe had not known loneliness before this period.
From the beginning of her life
she had been cradled
in the arms of those girls
and now, so many years later, she
yearned for them. Yearned
to go back there, knowing that if there was
no way out of this body, no way out of this
trap, no freedom from
the binding they had put on her, then—
she wanted to rot there with them, at least.

So Doe
ceased her wanderings and returned
home.

Back to the place
where she had been born, where her girls
died.

Half a century had passed
and the town was different but
the same—
roads still cracked, but wider now
and new buildings, new light
neon in the night.
But still
the same pervasive emptiness, the same
heavy air.

She traced a circuitous path around town.
The Mayweather house gone, but
the land there still
scarred. The space where the market used to be held
replaced with homes, sterile and
still.

The most difficult part was still to come.
Returning
to the farm, to see
what had become of the house,
the land,
the bodies.

So Doe set out
walking through the center of the town.
It was a quiet, ghostly night. The streets
wet, slick. Lights hanging above the roads
switching green to yellow to red,
back again.

That's when Doe saw her.
Bathed in red, standing
in the middle of an intersection. A girl—
brown skin, bare feet, in a
white dress.

For a moment Doe felt as though
the girl was an apparition. A
haunting. Not because she was there at all, but because
her face, the tilt of her chin, the shape
of her eyes—

it was like looking right at Bonnie.
Impossible but true.
Bonnie, always Doe's favorite, the one
she mourned the most, the one
who named her.

Doe moved a little closer
to the girl—what harm could it do? The girl couldn't
see Doe, and it seemed like perhaps she wasn't seeing
anything at all. A waking sleep, a sleeping
walk.

This girl, she was
beautiful. Muscle
like she could fight, wide eyes and full lips
in a heart-shaped face
angelic, like she would never dare hit anyone,
although the bruises on her legs
said different.

Doe took a long last look, a

small memory
to add to the endless collection.

Good night, Bonnie,
she said—

and the girl looked up.
Deep dark eyes
gazing directly at Doe.
"What did you call me?" she said,
curious,
velvet voice.
"My name isn't Bonnie. It's
Maris."

15
TEAM

Monday.
We are on edge,
anticipating, waiting.
She's here, isn't she.
We can smell her.

We push thoughts of her down so we can get through the day,
make it to practice,
and we are walking the halls from homeroom to first period when
there she is.

Slick of blond
stroke of short-skirt girl
gliding
between and around and through
like there's no one surrounding her
or like whoever's there
means
nothing
at all.

Promising,
we think,
and we disperse, scatter
not unlike pollen,
poison
on the wind.

She is in Claire's Spanish class,
takes chem with Violet,
English with Prairie.

Prairie, who watches every move Genevieve Ray makes,
where she chooses to sit
(third row)
how she answers her name
(slow and bored)
how she raises her hand
(wait—she doesn't).

Prairie takes in all of it and files it away
for later use, later recounting to us
because that is what Prairie does best
conditioned to please
chasing praise any way she can get it
because she sure as shit doesn't get it
at home.

We text, period before lunch:
Say hi?
Tell her to eat with us?
No we'll look like fucking stalkers—
—she's the only new girl in school today it's not like—
No, let's see what she does.
Yeah. I wanna know how she handles this.

This the cafeteria,
and that from Maris.

We take our tables at the back, as usual.
Watch for her to sweep in,
or slide,
or hide.
But she never arrives
and we mark that.

Could be she's afraid.
Could be she doesn't give a fuck.

"Could be she's with Coach."
Lo says it, and August pinches her
hard enough to make Lo tear.
"We'll see," Maris says. "Later, we'll see.
At practice.
Where it counts."

❖

*"One—
three—
five—
seven—"*

We yell beats
lock our hands
toss each other high as we can
ride the wave

*kick
tuck
twist*

fall into waiting arms

*catch
land
clap*

work our motions until Coach
is happy with our sharpness, our
precision.

We do all this
without letting her know
our curiosity
because where the fuck is Genevieve?
We were promised Genevieve
but she is not here.

It is not until we are in pyramid
stacked like delicate crystal,
interlocking limbs,
that the door flies open
hits the wall, *crack*,
and there she finally is.

Coach claps, that gunshot sound.
"Come down!"

We hit the ground,
bend and stretch to catch
our breath,
and Coach waves her over
pink nails flashing.

"Team," she says, "this is Genevieve.
Genevieve—
your new team."

-<->-

Your?
We bristle, set shoulders
and stare.

This is our team, Coach,
we think.
Ours. We made it,
us,
and
you.
Don't forget that.

Genevieve says nothing, only looks
somewhere beyond us,
somewhere we can't see.

"Genevieve, get warmed up," Coach says.
"The rest of you—
get back up there."

❄❄❄

One—
three—
five—
seven—

Heels in hands,
fingers around ankles,
dip and push and lock and hold—

one leg lifted, arabesque,
arms out wide,
smiles sharp and clean—

we are
performing.

For Genevieve, we are
putting on our best,
showing her what we have
because contrary to what this school,
this town,
believes,
we do have something.

Or maybe it's not performance.
Maybe it's a challenge.
Come on, Genevieve,
watching from the side of the mat,
heel tapping in time,
arms crossed.
Show us what *you* can do,
show us what makes you so fucking special.
What makes Coach say you're Good.
Come on, Gen, come on.

⊰⊱

Genevieve readies herself in the corner of the mat.

We see the steadying breath she takes,
the chest lift-fall preparation.

And then she explodes—

A powerful run leading into a
roundoff,
hands barely grazing the mat
before her feet come back down
and then a
back handspring
into

whip,
whip,
full twisting back somersault—

Fuck, we start to whisper, *holy fucking—*

—and she doesn't stop,
returning the way she came,
punch front step-out right after the full,
another roundoff,
back handspring,
whip,
back handspring again,
double full twisting somersault
to finish.

And she is perfect in the air,
every time,
hips lifted,
knees locked,
toes pointed.
And chest high when she lands,
always ready
for what comes next.

Genevieve turns to Coach.
They are both all smiles,
arms outstretched
for the hug
we never get.
It's not appropriate, Coach always says,
but somehow today it is,
for Genevieve.

But we see, at least.
Something Coach sees.
The girl is Good.
We see it.

⏤⟨⟩⏤

Of course we steal glances
as Genevieve showers, changes,
brushes her long wet hair till it hangs straight.

Up close we can see
the blemishes absent from her social media photos
but that ski-slope nose
is still perfect in real life.
She is leaner than us,
fighting form,
muscles shifting under white skin.
Except the chances that Genevieve Ray
has ever gotten into a real fight?
And we can scrap like the sharpest feral alley cats.

She has yet to speak,
and don't think we haven't noticed,
don't think her
power
precision
punch
have gotten her off the hook.

August is the one to sit beside her.
"So," she says, "did you cheer before?"
(As if we don't already know every answer.)
Genevieve shakes her head.

"Gymnastics," she says, and the voice that emerges
is soft ocean breeze
(we guess; we have never been to the ocean).
"Elite level. But I quit. And we had to move, so . . ."

The end of that:
so now I'm in this dead-end shit stain of a town
cheering
instead of
competing.

"Why did you quit?"
Claire asks.
"How come you moved *here*, though?"
Kate asks.
"Are you liking it so far?"
Cami asks.
"How do you get your back tuck so high?"
Lo asks. "I always feel like I'm about to land on my face
and—"

"Jesus, let her
breathe," Prairie says,
and so we all
exhale
take a step back
still watching Genevieve
waiting for her to
answer.

Genevieve
crosses her legs and
looks around the room

at all of us staring
a small smile on her lips.

"Curious,
aren't you?"
she says. "I quit elite gymnastics
because I wasn't on the Olympic track."
She is
ticking the answers off
with her fingers. "We moved here
because my dad got a new job
nearby."
She points at Lo. "*You* need
way more power
to fix your back tuck. All your tumbling,
actually. And as for
if I like it here—I mean.
What is there to like?"

August looks at us like
cool it with the questions, bitches
and nods at her.
"It's not so bad here," she says.
"Well. No. It's hell on earth. But—
we have each other." August slides
fingers along
the bench,
the space between her
and Genevieve, and then uses that same hand
to gesture at the locker room,
the gym beyond. "We have
this."

We watch Genevieve for her response
but she just finishes packing her bag
and stands.
"Guess we'll see," she says.

<-+->>

August looks at Prairie,
who looks
at Maris.
That's supposed to be *our* line.

"Gen."
Maris calls to her
finally
as the girl heads to the door.
"You hungry?
A few of us
are gonna go eat.
You down?"

We give her our best smiles,
pretty bitch smiles,
come see the darkness with us
smiles.
We each remember whose smile reeled us in
gave us the idea to try out in the first place.
Who told us that yes,
this place was for us,
these girls
were our family now.

Genevieve looks over her shoulder,
dark eyes.

"Thanks, but
I'm busy. Oh, and—"
Here she clicks tongue against teeth,
looks Maris up
and
down.
"It's Genevieve.
Got it?"

16
GENEVIEVE

Genevieve rounds the corner and stops.
Sinks back against the wall
and breathes, finally.
It's suffocating
being in there with them
those *girls* that *team*
the way they stared
the questions
how they talk and move and watch
like one organism.
How they all looked to the captain—
Maris—
for her approval, like they couldn't
form their own opinion
without her
and how she had tried to reel Genevieve in
the look on her face when Genevieve turned her down
corrected her name
the hard glint in her eye
like how *dare* she not want their nickname how
dare she not want to go eat with them
like what, does she have somewhere *better* to be?
And if she weren't afraid of not being able to breathe
Genevieve would go back in there and say
no, I have nowhere better to be and no friends here and
no one I know besides
Coach
but I don't know how I'd eat with you all
when you make my skin crawl.

She looks up at the gray sky
the lone bird wheeling around.
I could quit
she thinks. Could walk back into Coach's office
and say *hey I know you bypassed usual procedures*
to put me on this team
and I know you warned me about them
but now that I'm here I see them
and I think I don't want to be part of this.

Except Coach *did* do something special for her
because she knew Genevieve would need something
and there's no good gym around here and no gymnastics team
at this school
so this is the next best thing
and *god* it did feel *so* fucking *good* to be
throwing her body around again
using all the skill she has to show off
waking something up
and even now, even though she still feels as if she's pulling herself
out of the team's dark morass
she can also feel
the fire in her belly, the
bright sparkly *alive* feeling she only gets
when she touches the mat.

She straightens
flicks her wet hair back
takes a slow, deep breath this time.
No. She won't quit.
They'll want her to
when they realize she's not interested in

whatever symbiotic, codependent
relationship they all have going on
but she won't
and they'd better be careful.
If they push her too hard
they'll see what it's like when a girl fights back.

17

MARIS

"She's a fucking bitch."

Maris spits it at Nell
around the burger in her mouth
and waits.
They are in a booth
at the back of the mostly empty diner,
the girls up at the counter
pretending to flirt with the kid filling sodas
pretending not to listen to Maris and Nell's conversation.

Nell looks at Maris. "So
she didn't want to hang.
It *is* her first day.
And the team, you're . . ."

Maris knows
what Nell isn't saying
because they've had this disagreement
before.
The team is *too much* and
Maris gives them *too much* and
if she would think about the team less
spend less time in the gym
then maybe she would be doing better in school
maybe she could think about *herself* more
and the future that's out there for her.

The thing Nell doesn't understand
is how much Maris
needs

the team.
Maybe if Nell
actually *loved* her
then Maris wouldn't need them so much.
Has she ever thought about
that?

Maris shakes her head
refocuses. "So what if it's her first day? She should at least
make an effort," she says.
"She's on the team, but
it's like she doesn't want
to be here."

Nell laughs, sharp.
"None of us want to be
here.
Shouldn't that count
in her favor?
She's the same
as all of us."

Except you *aren't the same as us,*
are you? Maris thinks.
That's their whole fucking problem.
Nell, who thinks the team is *stupid*, really
Nell with her academics
and nagging Maris about tutoring
Nell, who already has plans for her college applications next year
and the future where she leaves West Eaton
and wipes it from her mind.

Maris looks away. "Sure,"
she says,

"she's stuck here, too. Let's give her a
gold fucking star."
Then she laughs. "Makes up for those medals
she's not getting anymore."

Nell finishes her fries
and stands to leave.
"Fine, fine," she says.
"Just—don't ice her out.
Think about how it will look
to Coach, at least."

18

TEAM

As much as we hate it—
Nell is right.
We have to be careful
think about how whatever we do
will look to Coach.

Gen—
sorry, *Genevieve*—
is Coach's best girl.
If this wasn't clear to us
on her very first day
then the next weeks
show us.

Practice used to be
Coach, clipboard, steely gaze,
us sweating out
our self-loathing
while she worked us.
Trained us and kept us tight,
in our minds,
where we needed it.

She knows what we do when we leave the gym.
She knows who we are.
What we go home to.
Nobody.
Parents out late,
working
drinking
fucking.

Taking care of
siblings,
taking care of
ourselves,
except all that means is
we make food in the microwave
and put ourselves to bed.

So she was hard
on us
harsh
with us.
At tryouts every year
she says the same thing:
"I will make you work
hard
but you will learn
to enjoy it. When you make a mistake
I will tell you how to correct it
and you will do it again
and you will do it right
and you will feel like there's nothing you can't do
if you push yourself.
No matter what else is going on
out there"—
here she jabs a finger
toward the outside world
the same gesture every time
the same passion—
"in here, in this gym,
you can put all that aside.
In here you will learn that
there's nothing you can't do
if you really, *really* want it."

We believed her
and she did
exactly what she said she would.
We needed a home and Coach made that for us.
She became that for us.

Now Coach is different.
Now practice is
Coach, clipboard, and Genevieve
at her side.
Genevieve giving tumbling tips
Genevieve whispering into Coach's ear
and it feels like no matter how hard we push
how well we take Coach's corrections
we can't stop disappointing her
by not being as good, as polished, as perfect
as Genevieve.

But it's not our fault
that we didn't grow up in Coach's hometown
train in her gym
know her *before* she was Coach.

We stretch before practice.
Genevieve walks in with Coach.
We shower after, get ready for work—
Genevieve catches a ride in Coach's yellow VW.
We never knew Coach well, don't know
who she dates or what she likes
and before, that was fine, boundaries, a little mystery around our
feared loved leader

but now, as the weeks pass, as the ghost of Halloween
disappears behind us
and the tension of Thanksgiving with distant relatives
looms,
as Genevieve
becomes a permanent fixture—

we don't feel special anymore.

And what are we supposed to do with that?

19

TEAM

"—and if you drop that stunt again, Lo,
you will be gone," Coach says. "Am I
clear?"

Four weeks after Genevieve's arrival and
we are behind the bleachers,
freezing in November's misty drizzle,
long-sleeve black tops
under our
green-and-white uniforms,
flesh-colored tights beneath our
skirts.

Of course Coach is clear.
Haven't we been
telling Lo
to lock her knee when she's up there,
when we're holding her above our heads?
Haven't we been
telling her
to strengthen her ankle?

She doesn't listen.
Well.
She doesn't listen to *us*.

❖

Whistle screams on the field.

Genevieve puts her hands on Lo's shoulders.

"You got this," she says,
a devious smile on her face,
as if she believes we are
the kind of girls
who platitudes work on.
Well. Clearly Lo is
that kind of girl
because she's nodding
staring up at Genevieve
like she is an angel sent to save her.

"But what if I don't?"
There's a tremor in Lo's voice,
one
we have all felt before,
kept deep inside.
Letting it out shows
weakness.
We didn't have long enough with Lo
to make her strong enough to keep that tremor inside
to make her strong enough to resist
Genevieve and her fake help.
It is so obvious to us
that Genevieve is fucking with Lo
fucking with *us* by fucking with Lo
and yet whenever we have tried to make Lo see the truth
pulled her away from the wolf in our midst
given her *our* advice, the advice that should matter *most* to her
warned her that Genevieve cannot be trusted
she has always gone running back.
We see them whispering in the locker room
and stretching together at the end of practice
and smiling at each other in the hallway.

She is a black hole
and Lo's little star
cannot resist the pull.

"What if I don't have it?" Lo is saying now
oblivious to our hands reaching for her
taking a step closer to Genevieve.
"Coach is gonna cut me."

Genevieve shakes her head,
pony bouncing.
She is a mass of curls,
bow new and stiff,
her red lipstick a
violent slick. "That's not going to happen.
Everything's gonna be fine. You're gonna be
perfect."
She smiles again
past Lo and at us this time.
"Trust me."

⦉⦊

On the sidelines we
glow.

We have perfect bows,
shiny lacquered lips,
pristine white sneakers.
It is our ritual,
getting ready.
Hair, makeup, uniform on,
hair spray to stick your shorts to your thighs,
no flash of ass here.

Tape up knees, wrists,
whatever you need.
Cloud each other in perfume
soon to be overcome by sweat,
the best smell there really is.

We hit beginning pose,
chins up, smiles tight,
the sheen of pride, these
uniforms, these
girls.
Us.

⫸⫷

Genevieve probably got ready at Coach's.
Bitch.

20
TEAM

Lo falls.

⪻⪼

By Monday she is gone.

⪻⪼

We can hear her sobbing
in Coach's office
as we change.

Move quiet, letting her be heard.
See how easily it could be us, how
close
we are to the edge.

Then again—
it would never be us like this.
We would never be so weak
as to let ourselves be
manipulated
by the new girl on the block.

If Lo had just listened to *us*
to her *real* friends
then she wouldn't be in this situation
either.

Genevieve slams her locker,
cracks the air.
We stare at her

not with awe but with something
like it, something
that makes us hate
how simple her plan was and how
she pulled it off so
flawlessly, so
easy.

"She'll be fine," Genevieve says,
sauntering to the exit.
"This shit is
tough.
Some girls
just can't handle it."

21
GENEVIEVE

Tuesday practice
and Genevieve flicks her tongue out
tasting sweat on her lips
as she readies herself
one foot on the mat
the other locked in her teammates' grip.

It was almost too
easy
to pick Lo off
but what matters is that
she showed the team.
She showed
Maris.

You are not the only one with
power
around here. See what I can
do to your girls?
See how
easy
that was for me?

Sure, this
is not exactly what Coach had in mind
when she put Genevieve on the team, but
she *had* said that Genevieve being there
would show them how much further they could
push
themselves, and that was all

she was trying to get Lo to do
right?

Don't be afraid to
show off.
Coach's exact words.

So, there. A little
display
for them all. A
reminder
that they shouldn't be
too comfortable. A message
that she isn't scared of them
that she isn't going to run
but isn't going to
give in
to their strange ways
either.
She's going to be on this team
her way
and if they don't like it—
they'd better fucking act like they do
or who knows which bitch
I'll take out next.

Up front Coach claps
counts them in
and Genevieve can't help but laugh
as she is propelled high into the air
soaring.

22
TEAM

"Hold it, hold it—
good, Gen! Very nice."

We sweat beneath her, hands cradling her ankle,
glance at each other,
same hard stare.

She's perfect
in Lo's place.
Nails it every time.

⤙⤚

Don't ice her out?
Fine.

Then we
will
burn
her
down.

23

TEAM

We are bored.
Without Coach's attention
we feel ourselves changing.
Our bodies expand,
bones,
blood.

We ride with heads out sunroofs,
arms stretched out open windows,
in lashing rain and ice,
a new way to maybe feel something
stinging.

We steal trinkets
from our jobs,
scarves and earrings and little glass bottles of things
shoved into bags.
We hide our smiles as we pass the security guards,
toss each other our spoils
in the back of the car.

Never were good little schoolgirls before, but now?
No attention, constant detention,
failing grades.
Our teachers hurl *what is wrong with you?* at us
in every class
but we only want to hear it from Coach
want to be called into her office
and have her look at us
with her dark, dark eyes
like she *knows* we can be better than this

and we want to promise her that
we'll try, we swear

but now
when Coach calls any of us in
it's not to talk about our grades or our
behavior
but what we do on the mat.
How Violet's jumps are sloppy
how Cami's leg needs to be higher in her arabesque
how Prairie needs to clean up
her choreography.
"Watch Genevieve,"
she tells us, tucking her hair behind her ears
showing off her neat little silver hoops
so much nicer than the cheap shit we wear.
"See how she does it, and then
do it better. Okay?"

What is wrong with us?

How about:
We put all of ourselves
with all of our failings and all of our flaws
into Coach's hands
and she promised to
care for all of it,
care for us.

How about:
She pays so much attention to her
golden girl
that it feels like we have become
invisible?

How about:
In the second week of December
winter break almost in touching distance
and only two weeks after she cut Lo,
we watch Kate get pulled into the office
see her twenty minutes later, in the locker room,
red-eyed.
"I'm out," Kate says, and we
gasp, we
stroke her back, her shoulders, her cheek.
"She said my tumbling isn't good enough
anymore."

How about:
Coach does the unthinkable
in our last practice of the week
when we're already tired
dreading the shifts waiting for us after
holiday rush
in full swing.

She is standing watching us in formation
one hand on her hip
the other sketching the air, ideas
we can't see
and we're enjoying the brief respite
to catch our breath, but then Coach
looks at Maris and says,
"Maris. You take Kate's spot.
Then Genevieve—
you come up front."
She points to the spot between Prairie and August,
where Maris currently stands.
"Right here."

24

MARIS

Maris blinks slow, all of her
going slow,
because that is the only way to explain
how she just heard Coach
giving her spot away to Genevieve.

"Are you kidding?" Maris glances
from Prairie to August, to Coach. "No.
This is my spot. I'm captain. I
earned this."

Coach lifts one eyebrow,
the calm control of it
what always chills Maris.
"Exactly," Coach says. "You
are captain. That means you
are the backbone. We've lost
a few bodies, and so we have
weak points.
I need you
to fill those weak points. Be the
backbone,
Maris."

She tosses her hair back, a deep dark
wave threatening to knock Maris down. "Or
did you think that captain
was a glory position?
Because if so,
I can find somebody
to replace you there, too."

It's not about glory.
It's about respect,
the blood and sweat
Maris has put into this team
to be rightfully rewarded,
captain,
except now Coach says she can take it away.
Just like that.
Like the past couple years mean nothing,
like everything Coach told her
only two months ago
about *why* she gave Maris captain
means nothing.

Feels like Coach is punishing her now
not for slacking off or shitty grades or weak tumbling
but for the crime
of not being Genevieve.
And even if it's not that
even if this is just Coach's way of
reminding
Maris of her responsibilities—

can't she find a way of doing that
without giving the spot Maris
worked her ass off for
to the fucking new girl?

That's what is on the tip of Maris's tongue
as she steps back,
a slow and sullen submission
although her body burns

with a scream
she fights to swallow.

⋘⟷⋙

"You're right, Coach."
Maris works her mouth around each rotten word.
"I'm captain. I keep the team together.
I'll go
where I'm needed."

Maris can feel Genevieve staring at her
the supercilious smile on her face.
Oh, she acts like none of this means anything to her
but somehow she's still winning.

Coach claps her hands together now,
that gunshot she loves so much.
"Good. Gen—"

And Genevieve glides past,
elbow catching Maris's hip.

Fuck you
she thinks,
but Genevieve glances over her shoulder
as if she heard exactly what Maris
wanted to say.

Maris holds statue-still,
her gaze locked on Genevieve's.

25
TEAM

What is wrong with us?

How about:
Everything was fine
before *she* showed up
and ruined it all.

LEGACY

It did not take long for Doe
to put the pieces together.

During the binding
all those years ago now
hadn't Iris said it?

No other human but those of us here
who gave our blood to this spell
and our descendants, who will share our blood
and our sacred connection,
will be able to see this creature.

Truth be told
Doe had almost forgotten about this clause
never thought too much
about descendants
because after all, the girls had died so young
frozen in amber before motherhood
could have entered their lives.

Except for one.
Bonnie.

The whole reason Bonnie had run away from home
and ended up at the farm, in the right place
to find Doe, was because of
the baby. Bonnie had already given birth
to a child. A daughter, who was
taken away from her
before Bonnie could even say goodbye.

A daughter who had grown up—
had a daughter of her own
who had a daughter of her own
who she named Maris.

And here that magical daughter Maris was,
decades later, staring
Doe in the eye, gazing
in wonder
like a child.

BEGINNING

It was late summer when Doe
and Maris met. The girl was
a sleepwalker
but she carried out full conversations
shared laughter and secrets with Doe
as if she were wide awake
eyes bright
voice clear
but still asleep enough
to not fear Doe
to not think it strange
that she was *talking* to a monstrous *deer*.

"I know she loves me, but
I wish I didn't have to
act like I'm *her* mother. *She's* supposed
to take care of
me," Maris said, telling Doe all about
her mother
as they walked the nighttime streets.

"She never says that she thinks
she's better than me, but
she doesn't have to. I can
feel it," Maris said, telling Doe all about
the girl she loved
as Doe watched her swinging from playground equipment.

"I have this dream
where I'm in *Rome*, and I have a

whole life there, and I'm a
completely different person
than I am now. I would have to be,
to make it all the way
to Rome," Maris said, telling Doe of
the future she fantasized
as they lay in a field absent any flowers.

Doe responded joyfully to each and every conversation—
how sweet, after all this time, to have
a friend in the world! How wonderful, to hear her laugh
that sounded so like Bonnie's! How electric
to finally be *seen*!

I think you will make it
to Rome, or
wherever else you want to go. You have
the entire world at your feet.
Make the most of it.

Doe tried not to let
the bitterness she felt
seep into what she said to Maris.
Rome—a different city, in a different
country, a place Doe had
never heard of before, a place Doe
could never dream of seeing
trapped as she was.

She was careful, too,
not to get carried away when she spoke.
Not to let slip tales
of the girls on the farm, of
Doe's own origins, of Bonnie

and Maris's connection to her.
Some sense told Doe to hold back
to let Maris believe this was all a dream
within a dream.
Who knew
how Maris would react
if she knew Doe was *real*?
If she knew the history of
where, who, Maris came from?

So she let Maris do most
of the talking
and her ears pricked
when Maris spoke about
the *team*.

"I'm captain now.
That means they have to do
what I say—but they do that
already. Anything I want
they'll do it," Maris said, telling Doe all about
the girls who seemed to worship her
as the moon glowed huge in the sky
and something stirred within Doe.

So she followed Maris
when she was awake
and saw them: the
team.

They were a wild pack
so vastly different from Doe's own girls:
They didn't hide, didn't
sequester themselves away, fearing

how others might see them, what they might
do to them.

No: This *team*, the girls whom
Maris was surrounded by at all times,
ran so free.

Throwing each other in the air
under blinding white lights.
Swinging from playground equipment
sharp words across the metal bars.
Lighting small explosives
that skittered and sparked through empty streets.
Running circles around town
with Maris leading the pack
her girls at her back, calling after her, following
wherever she led, the look of
pure adoration
in their eyes.

That adoration—Doe and Maris
have that in common. Maris was always
central. Maris
was the one they loved
worshipped
obeyed.
Doe had that, too, but also—
she served them.
Of her own will, most times, but only
because in the beginning
they had bound her.
Trapped her.

Late summer became fall
and
three things happened:

One: A jealousy began to burn.
Doe
was trapped, not only in a space
where nobody but now Maris
could see her, but trapped
in a body falling to pieces. She missed
feeling alive, feeling
vibrant. The sweat after a hard run, the
beauty she had once carried. Now she was
broken down, and she watched Maris
and the team
bursting at the seams
with energy. Oh,
what Doe would give
for such a life. For such
a body.

Two: A question began to build
in her mind.
A potential way out
of the quagmire she found herself in.
If her girls had used
sacrifice and ritual
to bind her, then perhaps the same could be done
to undo her. *To let me go
free.*

But Doe could not do it
alone.

She would need help. She would need
a willing sacrifice.
A new vessel.

And then—
three:
A buzz, amongst the team. A
new girl
had arrived.
"Genevieve," Maris said, late one night, the soles of her feet
blackened. She managed to make the name
bitter. Cold. "I hate her. I want to
destroy her."

Deep in Doe's tired mind
a new idea began to take root.

Perhaps
I can help you with that.

26

MARIS

It's a Friday night with no game
and they are at the gas station
picking up supplies.

Maris stands with August by the wine coolers,
still stinging
from that practice days before, from
Coach's words, the
look
she'd given Maris.
The rest of them are outside
teeth gnashing and eyes rolling
hungry
in search of their next feed.

August leans against the refrigerators, the glow of the neons
casting her high cheekbones
in stark relief. "You're really gonna let Coach
demote you?"

"She did not demote me."
No, just gave away my spot.
"Besides.
It's not Coach I blame.
Not really."

August nods knowingly.
"She thinks she's so much better than us,"
and now they have slid back to Genevieve,
the true source of all their problems.
"And she doesn't even fucking care, you know?

We mean
nothing
to her."

Maris draws in the condensation,
smiley face,
two Xs for eyes.
We mean nothing.
"She needs to learn."

"Learn?" August repeats,
and her hunger is clear in that one word.
It is no casual act
Maris bringing August inside with her
Maris steering them back to Genevieve.
It's always easiest
to get August on board
with whatever Maris plans to do
and she knows she should feel guilty
for using August's feelings for her like this
but that's as far as it ever goes, *knowing*
she should.
The guilt itself
just never comes.

"Yes. She needs to learn." Maris tosses her curls,
half pinned out of her face,
a hair slide that spells out *DYKE*
in clear crystals against the darkness.
"This was ours before hers.
She can't ruin
what we built,
not without . . .
consequences."

27

TEAM

We are passing cigarettes
rolling blunts
when Maris and August slip out of the store
and we smile,
wondering what delights
they have liberated for us.

But Maris calls out:
"Change of plans. We need to pay
a certain thief
a little visit."

Prairie hops up
on the hood of some stranger's car.
"Right now?"

"Yes, right now," Maris says,
her eyes liquid, and we
snap to attention at the steel in her voice.
"But first
find out where she is."

⤙⤚

It doesn't take long
fingers flying over our phones.
Genevieve has posted nothing herself,
but she's easy to spot
in the back of other people's photos
posted minutes ago, location tagged:
Lake Ewell

"Silvia's," August says, like
of fucking course.
Silvia Gomez, queen of West Eaton,
host of a hundred parties we've never been invited to.

Not that that's ever stopped us.

"Oh, Silvia," Maris says
and now her voice crackles
with excitement.
Infectious, contagious,
and we begin to shift like we can't not move,
need motion to stay alert and alive.

See, Maris
is on our side now—
not that she isn't always
but from the beginning
we were suspicious of Genevieve
and Maris was firmly Team Coach
but Coach fucked up
and now Maris is going to let us loose.

Now we can put that girl
in her place.

⤙⤚

It's like a magic trick.
We carve a path through the party,
magnets repelling the classmates
who wrinkle their noses
as we pass.
Glass-framed little house,
not right on the water but close enough,

and we snag a bottle or two
as we crash through the scene,
calling Genevieve's name the whole time.

"Come out, come out!
We know you're here.
We just wanna talk.
Come on, Gen.
Why are you hiding?"

⊰⊱

We are outside now, back
in the cold but we have
each other for warmth,
booze for warmth,
rage for warmth.
"Genevieve Ray!"

When she sees us it's from
all the way across the yard,
but we see the way she rolls her eyes
even from here.

"What the fuck are you doing here?"
she calls over to us, already sounds bored.
"Y'all don't have anything
better to do? Like,
I don't know,
making sacrifices to the
god of sad bitches
or something?"

She thinks she's funny.
That is Genevieve's problem always: She thinks

she is everything we aren't
and that all we are
is nothing important.
That's why she is not
and never will be
part of the team,
not really.
Too bothered about
impressing her captive audience, these
kids we've known our whole lives
who only want her because
she's shiny new, enough of a distraction.
Kids who she'll endure
until she grows tired
and fucks with them
just like she did to Lo.

⊰⬝⊱

It's Maris who steps up to her,
eye to eye,
chest to chest.

We see Genevieve try
not to smirk.

"We don't want anything."
Maris tips her chin up, looks Genevieve
up and down,
the same way Genevieve did to her,
first day.
"And we especially don't fucking want you."

Genevieve scrapes hair behind her ears,
holes punched in each,

blue stones hanging.
"So you came
all the way up here
to tell me you don't want me?"
She clicks her tongue behind her teeth,
crooked top row,
too crowded.
"Well, gee. Thanks. You can
fuck off now."
"You don't get it."
This is Prairie,
eyes bright and a hand at her throat.
"You really just don't get it, and
I wouldn't care if you weren't taking Coach
away from us—"

"*Taking* her?"
Genevieve laughs,
showing the
wet red inside of her mouth.
"Jesus, do you ever
hear yourselves?"

"Do *you* hear *us*?"
Maris jabs at Gen's shoulder.
"Coach said we were getting a new girl,
and we trusted her,
we trusted that any girl she picked
would belong with us.
But then here you come,
and suddenly Lo's gone,
and Kate,
and Coach—
she can't see you

for what you really are.
And maybe to you this is a
game, a
joke,
but this is our
team, this is our
family—"

⊰⟷⊱

"Family?"
Genevieve doesn't laugh this time.

We shift, as one,
like always.
One organism,
one organ.

When she speaks again
her voice is venom soft,
slippery.
"You aren't a family.
You're just a group of girls
who live in the same town
go to the same school
and got put on the same team.
And one day high school is going to end
and what the fuck are you going to do then?"
she says. "No, really—
do any of you bitches
have any idea?
Do any of you care?
This is your whole life, right,
your whole stupid world.
And that's the difference

between me
and all of you.
Cheerleading is not my whole life.
It's something I do
to pass the time,
until I can get out of here
and do something better.
So sorry
that I have a life outside of this,
sorry I don't wanna be in your
codependent
sad cult. But I don't want
to be stuck here for the rest of my life
and none of you can see further
than the end of the fucking mat."

28
TEAM

When Maris hits Genevieve it's not one of those
soft, open-hand slaps.
It's a punch to the gut,
the only kind she knows how to give,
the kind we have all learned in our desperate years.

Genevieve whimpers,
satisfying pathetic sound,
and as she doubles over
Maris grabs her by the hair
and spits through gritted teeth,
"I don't give a shit what you do with the rest of your life
but if you keep on fucking with my girls
I will end you, you
spoiled
little
bitch."

<-<->->

She is almost down in the dirt,
knees giving out,
Maris's grip on her hair all that's keeping her
from completely collapsing to the ground.
And then Maris drops her,
and we feel the satisfying thud of her
hitting the earth, and then
a retch, her spitting
into the dust.
From up here she looks
better.

She looks as small
as we want her
to be.

⋘⋙

The music's loud again,
and we are louder,
euphoric as we link arms,
ready to dance our way back through the house
and out to our cars
abandoned on the road leading up to the lake,
and we're hands on each other's hips
shoulder to shoulder
triumphant because
this is what we came for and
now everyone will know
how unimportant Genevieve Ray really is—

⋘⋙

"You wanna *fucking* fight?"

⋘⋙

We thought she wasn't
tough this way

but Genevieve throws herself at Maris
and what a stupid idiot, we think,
when there are so many more of us
than there are of her

but then there are arms around our waists
the crowd of our classmates
finally getting involved,

hauling us off, holding us back
as a voice we know belongs to Silvia Gomez
screams, *"Someone get those bitches
under control!"*
until it's just Maris and Genevieve clawing at each other
down in the dirt

⫸⫷

we have never seen a fight so dirty

the two of them wrestle on the ground
and Maris cracks her fist across Genevieve's jaw
but Genevieve swings too, her knuckles
connecting with Maris's temple
and Maris is knocked back for a second
enough time for Genevieve to pin her down
arm across Maris's neck—

our elbows fly at the bodies holding us
screaming *get off of me get off*
a thrill running through us
each time we feel our bones
connect with a body
cheekbone, nose, gut—

somewhere beyond us someone yells *fight!*
loud enough to pierce the lake
and on the ground Maris brings her knee up
between Genevieve's legs
and pushes Genevieve off—

29
MARIS

Maris learned to fight when she was a little girl
but she never learned to fight clean.

Still can feel
where Genevieve's arm pressed against her throat
as she scrambles to standing,
beating Genevieve to her feet,
and shoves Genevieve back down to the dirt.
Dimly registers the phone flashes
but doesn't let that stop her
as she steps one foot on Genevieve's left wrist
and presses. "Have you had
enough?" she rasps. "Do you
get the fucking message yet?"

Genevieve smiles, bloody teeth,
and part of Maris wishes she would concede
but the bigger, sharper part of her
is excited
that she gets to do this now.

Maris lifts her foot, heavy-soled boot,
and brings it down with her full weight—

≺⟵⟶≻

But it never connects,
stays hovering midair
as arms circle her waist
and drag Maris back.

"What the fuck—"
Maris rips free, ready to go back in
but the crowd is fleeing
and over the music still thumping
the panicked shouts of her classmates
Maris hears the siren.

⤜⟷⤛

Maris wipes the back of her hand
across her mouth,
red lipstick and blood.

"You're lucky," she says,
noise of the siren creeping louder, closer.
She looks at her hand and then at Genevieve,
on her feet now,
one strap of her dress ripped free.
"But if I were you, I'd think
carefully
about showing up to practice
on Monday."

30
TEAM

We pull Maris by the arm—
"Come on, we gotta get the fuck out—"

back outside running
like everybody else is
running from the sirens and
running on a high

everybody loves a fight
we feel the electricity
the high of the night

see, they all claim
not to care about us
not to even really notice us
but when we show up
we always make it worth their while.

-<+>-

We are back in our cars
and on the road
before the cops even show.
All they'll find when they get there
is a hundred crushed beer cans
Silvia pleading ignorance
and the neighbors down the way who made the call
twitching behind the curtains.

We cruise with the windows down
August tending to the scrape by Maris's eye
the afterglow settling on us.

Maybe Genevieve learned tonight,
maybe she didn't,
but we got what we needed.
We got to feel.

31

DOE

Doe runs alongside
keeping pace with the car
tracks them all the way
to Maris's house
watches Maris emerge from the car
chin up
ever the victor.

Doe watched tonight
saw the team assembling
something vicious in their laughter.
Followed them out
to a dark lake
a glass house,
stared out from the trees surrounding the lake
as the team made sure everybody knew
they had arrived,
as Maris and the girl
Genevieve
fought down in the dirt
and Doe had fought a battle of her own
a desire to protect her girl
flaring deep within
the way she had felt with Bonnie
and her old girls.

She wants now
to run to Maris
make sure her injuries are nothing more than
superficial

to delight with Maris
in her victory.

But she stays hidden
stays in her spot across the street
in the darkness between two houses.
Doe has only shown herself to Maris
while the girl is sleepwalking.
Been careful not to
break the spell.
If she were to go to Maris now—

she fears the shock
revulsion
that might show on Maris's face.
She fears
losing
the only connection she has.
Losing
the hope of a
future
that is growing inside her.

So she waits
while Maris says her goodbyes
while the team drives away
while Maris disappears into her house.
The door will open again
soon enough
and when Maris sleepwalks out of it
Doe will go to her
then.

32
GENEVIEVE

She creeps into the house
and up the stairs, wincing
with each step.

"Honey?"
her mom calls out
from downstairs
unexpected. *Why is she
still up?* "You caught me! I was having
a sugar craving. Want to split
this ice cream with me?"

Genevieve pauses at the top,
clears her throat so that when she answers
it's with a bright, breezy tone.
"When *don't* you have a sugar craving?
Rain check on the
ice cream for me. I'm going to
shower."

She hears her mom
moving around the kitchen
the fridge opening and closing.
"Sure thing, sweetie. Don't forget
you promised to come shopping with me
tomorrow!"

"I didn't," Genevieve says. "Can't wait."

In her room she stands
in front of the mirror and fingers the

torn strap
of her dress.
Skims her hand
down her body
to press at the tender flesh of her abdomen
air hissing between her teeth.

It hurts, sure
the scratches on her face sting
(shit, how will Mom not notice these
tomorrow?)
and her wrist aches where Maris's foot pressed against it
but beneath that—

She is keyed up,
limbs tingling with
adrenaline.
She's never fought like that
before
and something about the animal nature of it
was exciting, was fresh and real and
instinctual.
Genevieve was taught to fight
with pointed looks
and whispered gossip
and now it all feels so false
because *that*—
she presses her thumb into a bruise forming on her thigh—
was real fighting.

She looks up
catches sight of herself again
and it's the smile on her face
that starts the warning bells ringing.

Look at you.
What happened to you?
Are you becoming
just like them?
All that talk about how much you pity them
and here you are
enjoying what just happened.

She remembers herself, on the ground,
slapping at Maris,
writhing in the dirt.

Sinking
literally
to their level.

The Genevieve who showed up
to that first practice
two months ago
couldn't have even conceived of getting in
a fight
but in the moment it had felt right,
necessary.

She tips her head to one side.
No—not just in the moment, because
even now
there is no regret, no
wishing she could take back what she'd done, no
shame.

She moves toward the mirror
and reaches a hand out to touch the glass
tracing the shape of her smile.

The me of two months ago
wouldn't have done it, but she
didn't know how fucking good it would make me feel
to land a hit on that bitch Maris.

33
MARIS

Sometime around midnight
Maris rinses dirt from her curls,
watches the grime slick
down her chest, over
her belly,
rivulet down her legs and
disappear, finally.

She'd slipped into the house
to find her mom asleep,
for once in bed
and not passed out on the couch.

There is a risk
that the sound of the shower might wake her

which of course Maris would never do purposefully.
Wouldn't want that,
of course not,
wouldn't be fantasizing about her mother
coming to check on her
telling her off for coming home so late
then softening when she saw the damage
saying
oh Jesus, what happened to your face?

That's the kind of thing Coach would say—
used to say.

Maris stops the water
probes her

split lip with her tongue,
the taste of blood metallic.

Of course Maris knows
that's not what Coach is going to say
when she finds out what Maris did.

It's what Genevieve deserved,
Maris thinks, her only defense.
And now she feels her heart
slowing some, her muscles
loosening.

Really, this is Coach's fault.
She brought Genevieve into their world
and fucked with the team dynamic.
She should have known
how things were going to play out.
She should have paid more attention
to all of them the past couple months
and not just her brand-new favorite.
If Coach won't give them
discipline
then this is what will happen.
I am captain.
The backbone.
Sometimes
you have to take matters
into your own hands,
Coach.

I'm just doing
what you taught me.

34
TEAM

First thing Monday and
the suspense, it's *killing* us.
Is she going to show?
Has she learned?
And Coach—
does she know yet,
what we did?

We hope
secretly, naively
that we might get away with it.
Coach won't find out
and Genevieve will take the hint and quit
and everything can go back to normal
like it was before we ever heard Coach say
that girl's name.

But Maris wears her marks
like trophies
no makeup to cover her split lip
or the scratches
down her cheek.

We look at her in
awe
and shake off our fear of being found out.
Wish that we had the same decorations,
wish we had gotten a hit in,
that we hadn't let ourselves be held back.

<-+->

The looks come first.
Sitting in class,
and we feel it, the
heat of eyes
on the back of our necks.

Then: whispers.
As we walk through the halls
and into the cafeteria,
wait in line for cold macaroni and
wilted salad.

We don't normally attract so much attention.
Not even in uniform,
not unless it's harassment,
comments from the football team we cheer for
about the color of our underwear
what they'd like to do to us,
but today,
people see us.
They see us.

⊰⊱

Builds all day, like the
hum of a broken bulb,
buzzing and buzzing and buzzing
until
it is too loud to ignore
and then

quiet knocks on the classroom doors.
Each of us summoned,
one by one,
to the gym.

35
MARIS

Maris is the last there, she sees.
Everybody else is already
scattered across the bleachers.

Wrong place for a meeting—
a punishment? Maris presumes that's
what's coming,
knew it was coming.
The principal is there, her brown face flushed angry,
the principal's assistant, tugging the tie on her wrap dress
like she is afraid of them, intimidated.

Coach stands
a little away from them,
arms folded and a look in her eyes that says
if she could kill them all right now
she'd gladly do it.

It's not my fault.
I did it for the good of the
team, for the good of
us.
Don't you want us to be
the best? Don't you see what we all are?
Don't you see she is not
our family?

36

TEAM

Maris sits beside Prairie,
and we watch her try not to look
the same way we all had to keep ourselves from looking
at Genevieve.

She's up at the back of the bleachers—
what, hiding?
The same way she's trying to hide
the marks on her face? Because we can see
the patch job from here,
the powder sitting on top of her skin.

And we forget for a minute what we're doing here
because it smells like practice,
like hair spray and sweat and the mats, which have a scent
all their own
and we've never seen the principal in here outside of games.
But then she barks out, "Look at me,"
and we do it,
because in here we do what we are told.

❮❮❯❯

We know what's coming, of course we do.
Word of Saturday night (video too) has made its way
around the entire student body and now
to the teachers, who have brought us here
to make an example of us, we assume.

Isn't it funny?

We are so good at what we do, we are so
disciplined in here, we show up
at games to cheer
and events to raise money for our teams
but we finally do something bad—
or we are finally *caught*—
and now we have their attention.

Quick to punish
but when was the last time
we got a word of praise?

❖

The principal stares at us as if
she's seeing us for the first time, as if
she doesn't know what to make of us.
"I would think you all know
what a privilege it is
to represent this school on a team. But
from the footage I have been shown
many times over
I have to assume you don't care.
Attacking another team member? Enacting
physical violence? It's
disgusting."

Oh, but when our running back
broke a kid's ankle with a shitty tackle
that was fine?
And when Patrick Malone
was crowned homecoming king
that wasn't any kind of comment
or tacit endorsement

of him
knocking out his wrestling opponent?

They think girls can't be violent, they think it isn't
laced into our veins
like the rest of the world?

"All of you, every single one, is already on
thin ice.
Your behavior is disrespectful
your grades are appalling
and some of you are supposed to be *graduating*
this year.
What are you going to do
out in the real world?
You're lucky the police didn't arrest you,
lucky Miss Ray didn't file a report—"

We bristle. Like she didn't fight back.
She has claws, that one. And
she started it, really.
We wouldn't be in trouble
if Maris hadn't hit Genevieve, and Maris only
had to hit her because
Genevieve just wouldn't listen when we told her
we didn't fucking want her.

⊰⟨⟩⊱

Principal keeps on talking talking talking
but we have heard it all before
disappointment
disgust
distrust

and so we watch Coach
the way her fists close and open
how she refuses to lock eyes with any of us
longer than a second.

If it were anyone but Genevieve
she would understand.
Be on our side.
She used to be
loyal
to us, the girls she made.

All it took was one girl to undo us all.

⤛⤜

Principal still talking and us watching Coach
so intently that
we miss it at first,
only realize what the principal has said
a sharp moment later.

"—one week's suspension, and this team
is suspended until further notice. That means
no games,
no practice,
no nothing.
You want to act like
a pack
of wild animals?
Then you will suffer the consequences."

⤛⤜

What she said
hits and sinks.

No more team?
No more *us*?

⸎

We explode,
like how we did
when Coach told us a new girl was coming.
Started there, all of this started there.

"You can't do that—"
  "—we earned our spots—"
        "—wasn't even on school grounds—"
  "—weren't wearing our uniforms—"
                "—suspend us without a
                warning?"
        "—she doesn't belong here—"
                "—she did it too—"
  "—you can't *do* that—"

⸎

Coach raises a hand.
And we fall silent, a
fast hush.
"She can and she will.
If you don't want the punishment
you should have thought about that
before beating another girl at a party."

That comes out hard, professional, and we think
there's no way that facade is going to crack
but then she says, "Jesus, how many times
can I say behave! Do better! How many times
have I *told* you?"

and she sounds so desperate
that we would throw ourselves at her feet
if we could.

Sorry, sorry, we want to say

but then also the ever-present thought:
You brought her here
it's your fault, too.

⊰⊹⊱

Principal lets it sink in
luxuriating in our shock
and when she leaves, finally,
we know she will tell her therapist
what a good leader she was today.

We filter to the locker room
clear out our shit.
Someone tries to say it's not so bad
and someone else pinches her so she cries out
because it *is* that bad.
Another team might say *we don't need it, we can still*
hang out, we'll be fine!
but we are uneasy already.

Cheer is—
the bodies, the pain, the tempo—
it's all we have
all that belongs to us.
without it

who are we?

And then Coach appears
in the locker room that she usually never enters
and says
"Maris.
Come with me."

37

MARIS

They are in Coach's office
and Maris folds her arms, refuses to sit,
ready to defend herself against the
personalized tongue-lashing
she's sure Coach has prepared for her

except that when she meets Coach's eyes
she doesn't look furious
only exhausted, and she's
shaking her head
dark hair swinging in front of her face
fingers pinching the bridge of her nose.
"Goddammit, Maris,"
she says. "What were you
thinking?"

Maris has spent all weekend
forming slick sound bites
so she says, "I was just
trying
to be a good captain—"
But she hears how weak it sounds, how weak
she sounds
and suddenly her eyes sting, hot,
and she realizes with horror that she might actually
cry.

Maris sniffs hard and blinks rapidly
willing the weakness away.
"It's Genevieve," she says next. "She just doesn't

fit
on this team, and—"

"You know why I put Genevieve on this team?"
Coach interrupts.
"Not just because I knew her, knew her family.
Not just because I knew she would be good.
But because I wanted to *push* you.
You were so
hungry
last year, working
so hard chasing that captain position, and then
it seemed like once you had it
the chase was over
and you were losing focus, losing
that *drive* that I know is in you.
I thought a little competition
would get you back to that version of yourself,
toward bettering yourself, but
here we are."
Coach takes a deep breath and
her gaze on Maris is
pleading.
"I put Genevieve on this team to make things better,
not to have you
destroy things. Maris—"
Now Coach holds her hand out
reaching across the desk
toward Maris.
"You can't keep doing this.
You understand?"

Maris can't meet Coach's eyes now
can only stare at her outstretched hand

those permanently pink nails
wondering what exactly she's supposed to do.
Take it? Put her hand in Coach's
and let Coach run her thumb over Maris's grazed knuckles,
or squeeze hard
like a mom holding her kid's hand
so her baby can't vanish from her sight?

Something primal in Maris
wants to reach out, too, but
a bigger part of her is confused,
hurt,
embarrassed, even,
because
Coach seems to think that Genevieve is a
gift
she delivered to Maris, so that Maris would stop
being a disappointment
and become some version of herself
that Maris isn't sure exists
that she thinks Coach has simply made up
in her own head.

Knowing that the past couple months
have been some kind of experiment
aimed at, what,
fixing Maris?

I'm so tired of being a
disappointment.
Why is it so hard for people
to accept the girl I am
and stop trying to force me into becoming
something I'm never going to be?

So when she finally looks back at Coach
she only nods once
and says
(a note of amusement in her voice
that she knows Coach will hate),
"Oh, sure. I understand."

And she spins on her heel
marches back to the locker room
where the only people who take her as she is
are waiting.

38
TEAM

When Maris saunters in
we hold our breath as one
watching Genevieve
watching her
wondering if round two
is about to start.

But Maris—of course, Maris—
is the one who breaks the hush. Says,
"Are you happy now? You
screwed us.
We're done. And all because
you wouldn't just quit."

—<—>—

Genevieve pulls her shit out of her locker
not much at all, not like us
who have built time capsules in these metal boxes.
No pictures
thousand bobby pins
stash of period supplies
bag of assorted pain pills
scarlet lipstick bullets.

She's zipping her bag
and we think she's not going to say anything
but she turns, hair spiraling around her,
and looks at us.

"You're blaming *me*
for getting suspended, when I didn't say shit.

I don't rat.
You brought this on
yourselves.
There were, like, fifty people out there
fifty phones taking video
of exactly what *you* did.
What did you think, no one would ever see?
Should have picked your place better.
Now we're all screwed."
She tosses her bag over her shoulder. "But sure, blame me
all you want.
We all know the truth."

⤝⤞

But when we leave the locker room
Coach is there, waiting, that sour lemon car,
electro seeping out the windows,

we watch Genevieve walk over,
and sure, we can see
the tension in her muscles as she approaches, the way she
slumps as she gets into the car
her head low
like she's anticipating the telling-off
she's going to get from Coach
how she should have risen above it all
not sunk down to our level.

And sure, we can see
Coach's hands moving
punctuating her words—we have witnessed it enough
to know it even from a distance—but it's all still
so *unfair*.

So what if Coach is yelling at her?
She yelled at us, but we don't get to
be driven home in the passenger seat of Coach's car.
And we flare, rage, because that's it,
isn't it,
we get in trouble
and Genevieve can say we're all screwed
but she gets to keep Coach
this relationship they have, this history
and it's not fair, who do we have
except each other?

Coach revs the engine and they
peel out, together, such overblown obvious allusions
to old movies, and we can't do anything but watch them go.

39
TEAM

Winter break for us is usually daring each other
to skate on the thin ice covering the lake,
and holiday meals shuttling from one tense household to the next,
and parties with kids home from college, back to their hometown ways,
and working extra-long shifts in our heels and demure dresses,
convincing aspiring mommy influencers from the rich town
where the mall we work at lives
that those leather leggings *($250)* go great
with oversized cashmere sweaters *($475)*
and ugly boots covered in too many logos *($1,050)*

but this year it is different
because we are let loose that Monday after the fight
a whole week before break
and we don't know what to do with all this extra time
without somebody to impress.

So we pierce each other's ears
with ice cubes and safety pins,
get so baked we don't know
who we are anymore,
hang out in the parking lot behind the
empty strip mall
showing off tumbling to each other.

⊰⊱

We don't have Coach anymore
watching over us
caring for us

so what does it matter
if we crack our skulls on the concrete
break our necks
tear ligaments?

It's something, at least:
the burn and slip
of cold concrete beneath soft hands.
Wondering if this
team suspension
will be up
once break ends,
or is this it?
Is this our gym now,
abandoned spaces
where no one hears us yell?

⟨⟨-⟩⟩

What feels good:
thinking of an entire two and a half weeks
without Genevieve. No
vicious smile, no
ponytail whipping us, no
anything.

And we think
maybe
after break she'll have
come to her senses,
realized this team is not right for her
realized she is better off quitting, cutting her losses,
putting it all behind her

we don't believe that,
but it is nice
to dream.

40
GENEVIEVE

Her parents have gone to bed
but Genevieve is still up, watching
the lights on the Christmas tree as they
fade
from pink to red to blue.
Her mom will take the tree down tomorrow
always wants to tidy all the decorations away
as soon as Christmas Day is done
and Genevieve is already planning to be up early
so she can be the perfect helpful daughter
and definitely not because she has been handed a
long list
of chores, as part of her punishment
for getting suspended.

She looks over at the dining table, remembers
Coach sitting there with a kind of
sorrowful look on her elfin face, across from Genevieve's parents,
taking some of the blame: "Things got
out of hand—I knew it would be a little bit of a challenge
for them to accept her—I never thought it would come to
this."

Her parents were still *very disappointed*, though
and Genevieve can't blame them
because up until this point she has been the shining example
of a good daughter
and now—
being on the team has changed her
in ways she couldn't have anticipated
and what is she supposed to do?

She stretches out on the carpet
and closes her eyes. Maybe she should
quit the team.
How much easier would everything be
if she just quit?

But like every other time she has thought about it
she remembers how good it feels
to be using her body the way she was trained to.
She remembers how good it felt
to hit Maris.
And if she quit now, then the team
would win.
Maris
would win.

Yes, being on the team has
changed her.
Maybe she's becoming more
like *them*
but
does that have to be a bad thing?
I see
potential
in them. I could really help them—
not like she helped Lo. Lo was
collateral damage
in her quest to show Maris that she was not
the only bitch with power.
But this time she could *really*
help them. They could become
more
than just the warm-up act
for other teams. Maybe there could even be

some trophies
in their future.
Wouldn't that be sweet? Wouldn't
even Maris
be tempted by the idea of that?

Genevieve opens her eyes now
watches the tree lights
playing over the ceiling.
No. She's not going to quit.
That is, if there's even a team left
for her to not quit—after all, there are still
ten days
before school starts up again, and who knows
if Principal Diaz will reinstate them
when they come back?

Genevieve hopes she does.
She is surprised by
how much
she hopes.

41
DOE

Doe watches
the team running wild
in the winter cold.
It's times like these
when she misses her girls the most.
All this freedom
that Iris and Bonnie and the others
never got to experience. Lives
cut short, for
what?
Revenge?

Revenge. Also the reason
partly
why the team is out roaming the streets
when they should be in school. After all, that was what
the fight
that Doe had witnessed—and that Maris
had relayed, that same night,
in her half-walking state—had been about.
They only meant
to put her in her place, Maris said. They never meant
for it to blow back on them.
Well, Doe thinks, it did
and now
here they are
on a Friday night, exchanging smoke
from pursed red lips
in that old playground they treat as
their kingdom

but which is really only
wasteland.

They swing off bars
and wonder aloud about what
Genevieve is doing.
"Bitch," they say.
"Her fault," they say.
"Couldn't just
quit when she should have."

What is Genevieve up to?
Doe wonders.
So she leaves the team
slips out from her hiding place
and takes off at a run, through
the fields and onto the road,
making twists and turns
until she eventually comes to the house
where Genevieve lives.

Doe has come here before. To
watch Genevieve, too; to make sure
she's the right one for the role Doe has in mind.
Even from the outside of the house
Doe can see that Genevieve's life is
so different from those of
the team. Neatly edged grass
and warm light glowing from inside.
Genevieve likes to run
and sometimes her mother watches from the window
like as long as she can see her daughter
she'll be safe

or at least that's what Doe has decided
it means.
It looks like Genevieve has a
nice life.
It looks like there is
love
there.

Doe lifts her head
at the slam of the front door. Here Genevieve is now, waving
goodbye at the door and
setting off, headphones in,
the tinny rattle of her music
loud enough to seep out
into the night.

She runs with
confidence, no
fear. As if nothing bad
could ever happen to her
even as she sprints alone, in the
dark
in an angry little town.

She is beautiful
shiny in a way Maris
and the others are not. The lift
of her chin reminds Doe
of Iris, her grit, her
determination.
Doe runs behind, follows her this way and that, until
Genevieve stops at the top of a hill,
breathing hard. Doe knows she will turn
and run home now, and

she has seen enough for tonight
so she takes off on her own
spends a few hours wandering in the quiet
taking in the stars
before she feels enough time has passed
that Maris will have put herself to bed
by now.

She is heading toward Maris's home
but stops a few streets before.
Because there Maris is
half-awake in the middle of the road again.

Doe marvels
at how Maris stays alive. Her sleepwalking self
shows no signs of self-preservation.

Come,

Doe says
nudging Maris out of the road
to something closer to safety.

What are you doing out here
tonight?

Maris sighs.
"Do you ever wish
you could be someone else? Maybe not
forever, just for
long enough
to know what it's like."

Doe smiles.

You should be more careful.
Getting in too much trouble.

Maris spits
on the cold ground. "It's
all *her* fault. Fucking
Genevieve. Ever since
she came along, everything has gone
to shit. And it's like Coach
can't even see it. I wish
Genevieve would just . . . *disappear*. Or maybe
if she smacks her head hard enough
in practice
she'll become a completely different person.
That
would be perfect."

She strokes Doe's face
as she talks, and Doe
flares her nostrils, a spider
scuttling inside the cavern.

Perhaps if you . . .
No. Forget I said anything. You wouldn't
want to hear what I have in mind.

Maris looks up
eager
greedy.
"Tell me," she says. "I think I'd do
fucking *anything*
to get rid of her."

42
MARIS

She's back in the same dream
the one where she meets a creature half deer, half death.

Standing in the middle of an empty road.

This time the creature
looks at her like it wants something
but when Maris tries to ask
she finds she can't form the words
her voice stuck somewhere
locked behind her ribs

so instead she holds a hand out to the creature
and it comes close
dips its head down
to rub against her palm, like
a mild-mannered cat.
Maris lifts her other hand
runs it over the creature's antlers
fingers brushing away
the shed skin of an insect as she goes.

See
she thinks
you just want attention.

The deer raises its head, adorned,
and fixes its milky gaze on Maris.

Just like you.

43

MARIS

Maris isn't sure how long
she's been standing in front of the open refrigerator
milk inside slowly sweating.

She lets the door swing shut
the light extinguished
and takes a moment to orient herself.
Blue walls, ticking clock—
yes. This is Nell's kitchen.

She pads back upstairs
too tired to really notice
the wet prints left by her feet
and slips back into Nell's room,
into Nell's bed.

Nell's parents are out of town
celebrating the new year with friends
so here they are, on the first day of January
curled beneath blankets
keeping the cold out.
A fresh start to a new year
except nothing ever feels fresh
to Maris.

She watches Nell
breathing, slowly,
dark hair across the pillow
slack jaw.

Maris used to tell Nell
You know we don't have to wait
for your parents to be gone
so I can stay over.
They're clueless.
Just tell them I'm your friend
and I'm sleeping over.
It's true, isn't it?

And Nell always says
she's not keeping her parents from finding out about Maris
but protecting Maris
from meeting her parents. That she doesn't want to
subject
Maris to her mom's prickly questions, to her dad
and his casual homophobia.

That's what Nell says
but Maris can't help feeling like
it's a lie, simply Nell
trying to make Maris feel better,
trying to make
herself
feel better
about hiding Maris.

Dirty little secret, Maris said once
but then followed it with a loud laugh
so Nell would know she was so totally kidding
so Nell would know she so totally didn't mean it
so Nell wouldn't know
how it bruised Maris on the inside.

Dirty little secret.

⊰⊱

But it's the only warm place Maris has.
At her house there's her mother
fading further and further away
so deep in the depression that sometimes Maris
has to shake her
hard enough to rattle her skull
just to get her to look up.

She's been thinking about
getting her mom some help, but
the reality is that paying for a therapist
would cost more than Maris's mall job pays
even with the tips she got this holiday season
and they don't have insurance
so in the end there's nothing to be done
and Maris wonders how long it would take
for her mother to turn to stone
in that same spot on the couch she's always in.

Usually when things are this bad
she is okay, because she has the team,
cheer,
Coach.
But now she is
cut off
and so all she has right now
is Nell

god, it's so fucking pathetic
Maris wants to slap herself.

‹‹•››

(She does, later, in the bathroom with the shower running
so Nell won't hear
the sting of the hit on her own cheek.)

‹‹•››

They are downstairs in the morning,
Nell cooking eggs
coffee brewing,
when Maris asks her.

"You know how to get into
school records, right? So you could probably
get into Genevieve's records,
right?"

Not sure what she's looking for
exactly
but if there's dirt in there,
something Maris could use—

Nell doesn't turn around.
"Whatever this is,
forget it. Don't you think
you're in enough shit?"

Maris sits back, elbows on the table.
Look at her.
Short shorts,
old gym tee,
making breakfast.
Domestic shit.

This is what she'll do for countless other girls,
the ones she'll meet at college,
her first job,
the one she'll decide to marry.
But for Maris, these moments
here with Nell,
they're limited. Timed.
They only last until graduation, Maris knows that.
A year and a half left on their clock.
Nell has to leave, right? And Maris
is not allowed to go with her.
She doesn't have to ask
to know that.
And she doesn't tell Nell
that despite what Nell might think
Maris *does* think about her future
because she dreads sharing it with Nell
only to have her say Maris is
doing that all wrong, too.
To have Nell look at the secret album in her phone
where Maris keeps all the pictures of the
cities
she dreams of living in
and hear her say "Oh, sure, Maris, this is all
super attainable, great plan."

I let you treat me this way.
I let you believe you're so much better than me
because maybe you are
but maybe I could leave you, too,
maybe I could be with August, who actually
loves me
but I won't, because she's not the one I want,
you are.

So I stick it out
your superiority complex and all the other shit I hate
because I love you
so the least you could do
is fucking help me
when I ask for it.

44
TEAM

Sunday before school starts back
and Maris summons us.
The playground feels too small for us,
but we wind ourselves around its rusted parts anyway.
We need a plan, she says,
a way to reinstate the team.

She's right,
like always.
Carry on like we were
and we'll lose cheer for good.
Lose Coach.

⤙⤚

What was it Principal Diaz said?
Oh, yes: We are
representing the school
and
setting an example
and
it is a privilege *to be on the team.*

Okay, then. If it's good girls they want
then good girls they shall get.

⤙⤚

We can do that
we have rehearsed it, at the glass box mall,
in our nice neat dresses
and fake shiny smiles.

So. We will be
Good.
Listen in class
hand in assignments
show up on time
in appropriate attire.

Give them no reason to
punish us
further.
They want submissive, docile, compliant.
We will
submit.

⸎

"What about
Genevieve?"

It's Prairie who says it,
voices what we're all thinking.

Can we be submissive
beside her?
Can we get the team back
if she's still part of it?
Can we contain the parts of us
that hate her,
that hate how much better than us
she believes she is?

August waves her hand in the air
like she's waving Prairie's concern away.
"She'll play along,"

she says, but she looks to Maris as she says it
like she needs confirmation.
"But that means we have to, as well.
Can't let her get to us.
You know she has Coach on her side.
We'll be the ones to
suffer,
not her.
Never her."

⊰⊱

Maris sits atop the monkey bars,
peers down at us as she picks
flaking paint from the metal.
"Don't worry about Genevieve. I'm
working on it."

She slips between the bars and
drops
light landing.
"For now—
let's play nice."

45

TEAM

Knee-length skirts
unripped jeans
collars that press close at our throats

we ransack our Work Clothes
and parade into school
Monday morning like a scout troop
ready to sell our wholesome cookies.

Sit knees pressed together
and hands neatly folded
atop our books, the ones we actually brought with us,
the pens we hold ready to
take diligent notes on
Hamlet
and
quadratic equations
and
the Civil War.

⫷⫸

We do this all week.
Sit nice, speak nice, look nice.

We don't
pop
our gum while our teachers yell, and we don't
cut
each other's hair in the back of chem lab, and we don't
kick
the legs out of the chairs of boys who call us slurs.

⫷⫸

Genevieve—
at first we think she's paying us no attention.
No comments, no looks, no
slow blink when we pass her
in the hall.

But by Friday
we catch her
sharp glance sideways
quiet contemplation

see it ticking over in her head
what are those bitches doing
what game are they playing now

⫷⫸

But she says nothing.
Keeps to her world
while we keep to ours.

And we keep to our word
as one week becomes two
then three.
Don't get angry when we see her and Coach together
even though Coach will barely look at us.
Even though it hurts deep down
a hurt that tells us
exactly how much we need Coach
exactly how much we have used her to replace
mothers who let us down
sisters we no longer have.

So we pretend it doesn't bother us
in the slightest.
We keep it together.
We can do this
we are such good girls,
the sweetest, nicest girls you'll ever meet,
perfect and pristine.

❡

So Genevieve stays quiet
and we stay good and

it's not peace, this
balance
between all of us. Her at one end of the high beam,
us weighing down the other.

Not peace but an avoidance.
Mutually assured destruction
if we collide.
So we orbit carefully
and it feels as if
life can go back to how it was before we
even knew
that Genevieve Ray existed.

❡

Without cheer we are lacking
not just discipline
but pain.
What replaces that tight burn of muscle,
the electric shock through our ankles,
the exhaustion in our shoulders,
the too-sore moment that comes in the showers

when we can't even scrub the sweat away
too afraid of the chain-reaction ache it will
set off?

⤛⤜

We make promises, though.
We will not turn to our old friends
no razors or needles or sharpened bobby pins
no closed fists to the head
no fingers down throats
no lighter flames held against skin until it bubbles
no blades slicing through thighs until the white fat deep down
splits open.

Good Girls don't do that,
that's what the grown-ups believe.
So as long as we want them
to believe in us,
we will abstain.

⤛⤜

We don't even break the speed limit.

46
TEAM

As January comes to an end
we can see our teachers
becoming unsettled by us, this new behavior.
But what can they do? Tell us to
stop? We're being *too* good?
Paying *too much* attention?

It's not our fault that we're finally giving them what they want
and they don't like it.

Besides—

⦉⟷⦊

—we're having *fun*.

At first it was boring, like stitching ourselves
into too-tight costumes
of girls we never wanted to be.

But it is fun to see the way people watch us.
Never paid attention before, not really, not the way you'd
expect
and now we cut a path through crowded corridors
across the cafeteria
whispers in our wake.

Want to know why we're doing this
want to know what happened to the
caustic cruel cheerleaders
and our short skirts
our bleeding eyeliner

want to know
how long is this going to go on?

⤙⤛⤜⤝

We want to know that, too.
Been a month already
but we can't risk
being punished further
by asking
and Good Girls don't ask,
don't rock the boat, right.

So we keep being good
and we bottle up the fights we wish we could have with our mothers
and the words we want to carve into our arms
the kissing we don't allow ourselves to do
and the daydreams we want to get lost in at school

and we promise each other, late-night calls
under blankets, the closest to rule-breaking we get
like kids at camp,
we promise each other we will hold on,
hold on, hold on, just a little while more,
iron each other's blouses and button them up
with pearl-pink nails.

We will go as long as it takes.

47
MARIS

Sitting on the hood of her car, listening
to whatever bird wheels above in a
crisp blue February sky and calls out
as Nell and Maris, wrapped up in Nell's moss-green coat,
kiss like there is nothing else.

Behind her back Maris's fingers are crossed.
Fuck, this isn't
Good Girl behavior,
but what the others don't know—

Nell rests her hand on Maris's thigh.
"I'm impressed," she says in a whisper,
"but how much
longer are you going to keep playing this Good Girl shit?
Aren't you bored yet?"

⤝⤞

Out of her *mind.*
Being good, playing by the rules,
it's more draining than anything.
But this is the way it has to be, Maris knows.

They need the team back.
She needs Coach back.

Feels like stalemate, standoff.
Who will break first?

Coach needs them, too, another thing
Maris knows.

Without them what does she have? She
pushes them, punishes them,
sometimes—
in the best mood on the best day—
praises.

She must be bored out of her mind, too,
Maris thinks.
Hopes.

She is counting on it.

⋘⋙

What she won't say to Nell:

Yesterday after school Maris found herself
walking to the gym
usual path, autopilot
and when she got there she saw Coach
saying goodbye to another teacher
going into her office
and closing the door behind her.

Maris was at the door before she could think
better
of it. Raised her hand, ready to knock
but froze there
fist in the air
Coach on the other side of the door
and Maris
too afraid
to make a sound.

Afraid that what she has done has
ruined
her relationship with Coach, that Coach
has really
washed her hands of Maris
this time.
No more lectures in her office, no more
trying to convince Maris to be better,
because maybe Coach has finally decided that Maris
is beyond help.

Standing there
trying to keep her breathing quiet
and thinking that she can't tell August about this
because she's supposed to be
in charge. She can't tell Prairie about this
because she's supposed to be
leading this effort. She can't tell the rest of the team about this
because she's *not* supposed to be
afraid.

And she certainly can't tell Nell
because Nell will only say *I told you so*
Nell will say this is why she's always warning Maris not to
act out, or to
think
before she does shit—
not just in cheer but everything
as if Nell forgets who Maris is
as if she thinks there's some grand life plan
for Maris to ruin—

and the real problem Maris has now
is that she's afraid

Nell has been right about all of it
all along.

⤙⤚

Back in the present
Maris swallows down any fear
and tugs Nell by the braid,
pulls her close enough to graze her
teeth along Nell's jaw and up to her ear
where she whispers,
"It won't be long now.
Trust me."

48

DOE

Doe is not sure
that her plan will
work.

She spent many years
wandering alone
and not using her powers for
anything at all. What
was the point, when everything she could do
was bound to nature? And the girls
for whom those powers had brought
life and abundance and joy
were burned up
dead. No one
to impress, no one
to help.

But when the plan started
to take shape, Doe
began testing her limits. Calling up
rain and wind, making
bright sun and watching
flowers bloom and stretch toward
the light.

And reawakening that power—
it has revived her
somewhat. Her rotten body
pulsing with energy once more, too much
to be contained by her failing vessel.

Reawakening that power—it only solidifies the desire, the
need
for something new. Fortifies
Doe's idea, and pushes her
to carry through.

She has never tried
a ritual like this before. All she has to go on
is the memory of Iris and the others, their
ritual
that bound her
in the first place. And she does not know
if this specific idea
is even possible, but after all, the girls bound her power to
nature. And what is more natural
than life? The human body is
nature.
Blood and organs and breath
are nature.
If Doe can control
wind and rain and sun
then why not this, too?

Perhaps it won't work. Perhaps
this is something far beyond her
capabilities.
But everything has lined up so neatly, so
beautifully: Maris and her sacred blood,
Genevieve arriving at just the right time.

Doe has been feeding Maris
for a month now. Whispering
the plan, telling her exactly
what she must do. Seeding it

so it grows in her own mind, becomes
an idea that she has, believes it to be
her own. A solution to
all her Genevieve problems.

And if it doesn't work—
No, cannot get too far ahead
of herself, cannot
doubt too much.
Doe has Maris on her side, and
her own power, her own
desire.
Together they can make something
beautiful.

49
TEAM

It is the middle of February and
it's almost end of last period, Friday,
when the message comes.
We are itching in our seats
ready to run home and rip off the costumes
spend the rest of the night searching
desperate
for some way to relieve the pressure coiled inside us
without breaking the rules.

But then the message comes
and we are plucked out of class,
summoned to the gym.

Walk the quiet halls
and try not to look too hard at each other
because the hope, we know,
is naked on our sad faces.

But really, haven't we been
so good for so long
that we deserve a little reward?

Same as before
sitting in the bleachers
Genevieve at the top
Maris in the front
the rest of us spread between

but this time it feels
like we are on the same side

and the crackling undercurrent
is not hating Genevieve, wanting her gone—
no, we have moved on
(shh, we have to let ourselves believe this).
Still don't want her but right now we
need her
because if we are about to get the team back—

she's Coach's golden girl
so she comes with the house.
We get that now.

⸘⸙

Principal Diaz isn't even here.
It's just Coach.
Just Coach, watching us silent with those dark water eyes.

We preen under her gaze, open-throat baby birds
waiting for the smallest regurgitated nourishment
and it's been so long since we felt the weight of her stare—
feels better than landing a perfect tumbling pass
or a smoke in the summer sun
or driving at eighty with no lights.

⸘⸙

Coach lifts her chin.
"Good work," she says, each word
carefully formed
and handed to us.

She noticed,
she saw,
she *liked* it.

"Principal Diaz and I have discussed it. Since
no charges
were ever filed, and since your behavior has
dramatically improved—
starting Monday, the team will be
fully reinstated."

She holds up a hand, but we already know
we are not to talk
not to react
and our mouths are pressed firmly shut for her.

Now she takes the time to look at each of us
individually,
a weight passing from her to us
in a long gaze.
A weight telling us
that yes,
she noticed
she saw
she *liked* it
but also that she knows exactly *why* we've been doing it,
that we haven't tricked her,
only shown her that in fact
we can be the better versions of ourselves
if we are willing to try.
If we have enough
at risk.

"I want you all back," she says,
"and I fought for you, but know this.
Any behavior
like we saw before break
and the team will be gone

for good.
This is dead serious, girls.

I am *dead* serious."

⊰⊱

Holding our breath
we wait to be dismissed again
to run to the locker room, where we can scream it out
sweet satisfaction at having succeeded

but we don't move.
Not until Coach does, tossing her hair back,
and then she gives us the smallest twisted smile.
The kind that says she doesn't *want* to be the bad guy,
we just make her play the part.

"Go on," she says, smile widening a fraction.
"Get out of here."

We rise and run
scanning each other's faces, seeing
the same smiles on all of us
a joy, a *relief*
reflecting in all of us.
And then we catch sight of Genevieve

and it's not as obvious
her smile not as wide as ours
not so naked, but—
there. We spot it
even if she's trying to hide it
the same joy
the same relief.

She is happy we are back, too, and
we wonder for
a second
what that means
what Genevieve we will face in practice
on Monday, if she has changed, if she is willing
to work with us instead of
against us, if we are entering a
new era—

but then Coach calls out to us
and we stop thinking about Genevieve.
"Better not be out of shape!
Take the weekend to get ready, girls. I expect
your very best."

50

GENEVIEVE

She enters the locker room with the others
carried along with them
but then she breaks away and runs
into the bathroom, where she shuts herself into a stall
balls up her fists and
silently screams
into them.

She hadn't known this was coming
hadn't been told by Coach ahead of time
so the excitement she is feeling now is
pure
and taking her by surprise with its
intensity.

Maybe it's just because it's been so long—
two months now, god—
and she can feel her limbs trembling
ready to get back on the mat and explode.

Or maybe,
maybe—
she is glad for a second chance.
Glad that her opportunity to be part of this team
is not over.
Maybe she is beginning to understand
how this thing can make you feel
like nothing else matters.
in a way gymnastics never could for her—
always so much pressure
so alone

every other girl at the gym
direct competition, smiling
at every step out of bounds, every
loss of balance.
Working against each other
never together.

She bangs out of the stall
and finds her reflection in the mirrors above the sinks
pink-cheeked and hazy around the edges.

Maybe she wants a chance
to show the others that perhaps
Genevieve Ray
is not a lone wolf.

51

TEAM

You should see us.

It's Friday and we are thrilled, thrilling,
so we make
hasty plans.

There's a bar we pass
on the way to our jobs, always dressed
so nice, so tasteful,
and this bar
calls to us with its ooze
of dirt and sleaze.
Where we really wanna be,
so tonight, that's where we're going.

⊰⊷⊷⊱

We shed our Good Girl costumes and
sigh
sweet relief
shimmying back into our skins.

Short skirts with jagged hems
tight jeans ripped in too many places
hair done hoops in lips slick
fake IDs in hand.

We roll out,
and we've missed it missed it missed it so much
the squeal of our tires on the road
neons strobing by

and the coyote yell we release as we speed
into the dark.

⊰⊹⊱

It's still early but this place is
rowdy,
and we are riled up,
tongues out to taste the air and each other,
sour shots slipping down our throats.

Line dance in perfect time,
Maris spinning around with a hat she stole
from some girl in the back, and we are
wild, truly, more than ever
because we are happy, maybe,
and it's rare we feel that, rare
we are allowed these moments but we did it,

we won Coach back, we took her back,
and
now we know, have learned our lesson:

If we're going to be bad
we cannot get caught.

52
MARIS

Maris is in the bathroom.
She wipes sweat from her face
watching in the grimy mirror
the mascara bleeding beneath her eyes
the wavering edges of herself.

They did it, didn't they?
She did it, didn't she?
Got the team reinstated
back in Coach's good graces, and now
on Monday, they'll return to the routine,
running their track
and slapping thighs
and catching each other before impact.

She leans her forehead against the glass.
Winning is sweet.
She wants it to be sweeter
but Nell wouldn't pick up,
wouldn't even text until Maris had called three times
and all she said was
soooooorryyyyy at this stupid dinner thing w my parents!! congrats tho

⊰⟷⊱

A banging on the bathroom door interrupts her staring
and Maris yells
"Fuck off!"
loud enough that it reverberates in the small space.

"It's me."
August, voice seeping through the door's wood panels.

"Let me in or
I'm gonna piss myself."

Maris cracks a smile.
Slides the bolt back.

⤜⟵⟶⤛

August slips in
and she is sweaty, too,
but when Maris thinks about it
that's the best way they know each other

that sheen and drip after practice
dancing after drinking too much
running away from stupid ideas
in the middle of the night.

"What are you doing?"
August pulls her shorts down and sits,
frowning up at Maris.
"Talking to yourself?"

"Always am," Maris answers,
smiling.
Tips her head to the side and runs a hand up the back of her neck
into her hair, curls matted in the heat of the bar
from all that line dancing.
August keeps her looser curls short,
falling over her forehead and into her eyes
but clipped all the way down in the back,
so the air, Maris imagines, hits her skin like a caress.

⤜⟵⟶⤛

"Prairie and Vi are in some
contest," August says.
She wipes, flushes,
shimmies her jeans back up.
"Who can steal the most cigs or
something." She hip-checks Maris
so she can wash her hands. "I told them,
find someone with weed, at least. Make it
worthwhile."

Maris watches the water stream over August's hands
and then how August wipes them on her shorts,
drag marks on her back pockets.

"You know what I think we should do?
Mushrooms. I heard Alexander McClaine has them,
and we could all go camping—or maybe not all of us,
I don't think the babies are ready, but you, me, Prairie,
Claire, Vi,
we could go trip out by the lake or something.
What do you think?"

<<->>

Maris moves fast
steps in front of August
and pushes her back, up against
the wall filled with scrawled messages,
and she braces her hand on the mirror.

It's so loud outside and yet
in here,
quiet,
so quiet Maris can hear the blood rushing

in August's body,
turning her chest dark rose red,
creeping up her swan neck.

Her pupils are wide
and Maris feels that power,
the one she used to have
over Nell
but Nell does shit like
refusing to answer her phone when Maris calls
and here is August,
her best friend August,
who loves Maris not in spite of what she is
but because of it
who always answers her phone when Maris calls
who looks good tonight in those low-rise jeans and tattered T-shirt,
sunset-orange bra shining through.

⤛⤜

"Mare—"

She puts a hand up against August's throat
no pressure, just
her fingers,
there.

"I think you wanna kiss me," Maris says.
"Don't you."

It's not a question.
But August still nods.
And Maris still waits for that nod
so she knows she can do it.

Put her mouth on August's
and take what she wants.

⤜⬦⤛

She is pliable, compliant,
in a way Nell never is
in exactly the way Maris always thought August would be.

She doesn't move
doesn't push against Maris
or take control,
just stays still under Maris's touch

makes a small noise in the back of her throat.

⤜⬦⤛

It's slow,
quiet,
and that is all it takes to tell Maris
she has fucked up more than she planned.

It's not like she hasn't thought about
this,
her and August.
Thinks about it every time she
feels August watching her, hears
that catch of jealousy
whenever Nell's name comes up, when she's around.

But thirty seconds ago, when she decided to do this,
she thought it would be hot and fast.
Instead—

it's like she can taste August's yearning
a sincerity Maris has never felt from her before—
or maybe just hasn't paid attention to.

She thought it would make her feel good
and now she knows she was wrong
and guilt is creeping up her throat
sick and sticky
so Maris
pulls away,
wipes her hand across her mouth
and forces herself
to look August in her eyes.

"Shit," she says,
putting on an exaggerated smile,
a small slur,
"I am so fucking drunk."

There's a flicker in August's eyes
the slightest twitch of her mouth
and then it's gone
and she rakes a hand through her hair,
rolls her eyes and says
"You're a lightweight,
Larsen."

You're a bad liar, Grimes,
Maris thinks,
but then she's past it, because
she doesn't want to forget that they are celebrating
and there's so much night left.
"Come on—"

53
TEAM

We lose track of time
space
each other
the limits of our bodies
the edges of our minds.

We are, for once in our lives,
young and free
no thinking about the homes straining with tension
the people who don't love us
the lack of future.

We're just cheerleaders, tonight.

54

MARIS

Vibrating out of her skin
she doesn't know what time it is
only knows that the girls are still dancing
and she hasn't seen August since she left her in the bathroom
that was an hour ago
maybe more
right?

She slumps in a booth and watches
the hip circles and raised arms and hair flying
and she smiles like a mother,
proud of her colts.
Everything is back to the way it should be.

Except that you kissed August.

Except that Nell doesn't love you.

Except that Genevieve Ray is still a threat.

⧳

Genevieve, Genevieve, Genevieve,
don't you ever fucking shut up about Genevieve?
She is nothing
and I am everything
I am I am
I am so much more than she could ever be
so shut up about Genevieve
shut up shut up shut up—

⧳

The bar is loud
and the air is sweetsour
and the girls are calling her, laughs that are pure mania,
and Maris looks at the address pulled up on her phone,
Genevieve's address,
and smiles into the blue light glare.

‹‹››

It's not enough,
what they have earned back.
Maris knows it will never be enough.

Genevieve will always be competition.
She will never stop being in the way.

Watching the girls
and feeling the warm slip
of alcohol haze on her brain,
her tongue,
feeling the warm taste
of August still,
Maris thinks—

Why compete at all?
Why am I trying so hard
to be better than what I am?

All this plotting
and planning
as if there isn't a quicker
and more efficient way
to bring Genevieve to her knees.

So, why compete?
Don't have to, if there's no real competition.
Don't have to,
if the girl has a nasty little accident.

55
MARIS

On Saturday Maris wakes up late.
She takes a handful of aspirin
for the headache
and for the pain in her left ankle.
Hates waking up
with these drunken forgotten injuries
but especially right now,
when she needs to impress Coach on Monday.

Will we still have practice on Monday?
Maris wonders.
After what she's going to do today?

⟨‹·›⟩

Of course Genevieve lives
in the only nice part of town.
One block, really,
where the houses have front yards
and big bay windows.

Maris raps on the door three times
and looks up at the sky,
clear ocean blue, midday sun high.
One of those days when spring
wants to remind you it's on its way
if you can just hold on a little longer,
gifting you a few warmer days
as a promise of what's to come.

It's quiet,
a calm hush emanating from the house,

but she hears footsteps soon
and then the door opens.

Genevieve in satin shorts
and white camisole,
picture of innocence.
And then she says, "Maris. What
do *you* want?"

⊰⊱

Maris has practiced.
Enough so that she is convincing,
enough so that it could be true,
and the thing is—

it could be true.
If things were different,
if Coach could still belong to her
and Genevieve wasn't stealing
the only person to ever care, really—

but that's not how it is.

⊰⊱

Maris smiles,
or the closest thing she can manage.
"What I want
is to stop this.
You're not going anywhere,
and I'm not going anywhere,
and the team is back now,
so you and I?
We need to figure out
how to coexist."

"Coexist?"
The tip of Genevieve's tongue
creeps out of her mouth.
"So, what, this is a sit-down
or whatever?"

Maris lifts a leg, showing Genevieve
the sole of her muddy boot.
"Not quite.
Come on. Get dressed.
We're going for a hike."

56

DOE

From a safe enough distance
Doe takes them in.
Captures them like this
an image to return to again and again:
Maris humming with an energy Doe can feel
ready to get to work
and Genevieve almost glowing
with how little she knows. The two of them
framed in the doorway
so fresh, so
vital.
A moment for Doe to remember
after everything that is soon to happen
on this day. A day she made sure
to dawn bright and blue.
Had to make it perfect
for Maris to take her next steps.

57

GENEVIEVE

"A hike?"
Genevieve folds her arms
screws her face up.
Last thing she expected today
was to find Maris on her doorstep
and certainly not proposing some kind of
team-building-bonding
hiking adventure!
"What," she says now, "are we going to, like,
commune with nature or something?"

Maris shrugs. "I think better
when I'm moving," she says. "And we can't
be in the gym on a Saturday, so . . ."

Genevieve leans against the door frame.
Actually, if she called Coach right now
and asked to get into the gym
Coach would probably let them. But
Genevieve knows telling Maris that
would only piss her off, remind her
that Genevieve knows Coach better than her.
And that wouldn't be in the spirit of
what Maris claims she's here to do,
would it?

She eyes Maris.
Does she believe her? That Maris is here
to stop this thing between them, to squash the

rivalry and figure out how to coexist?
It doesn't seem like something the Maris
Genevieve has come to know—
the Maris who held her foot over Genevieve's wrist, ready
to smash it—
would do

but then again
that was before the suspension
and two months have passed
and if that was enough time to turn Genevieve from the
girl who thought the team was just a way to pass the time
to the girl who screamed with excitement
when she learned they were back
then maybe Maris is telling the truth.

Besides—
what Maris is asking for
is something Genevieve has already been thinking about.
Yes, the team is back now, but
there's no way to move forward
if she and Maris can't find some sort of peace.
Didn't I wish for
a chance to show them all that
I understand now?

And here is Maris
offering up that chance
on the kind of false spring day
that might as well have
clean slate
written in the clouds.

Genevieve exhales loudly.

"Fine," she says. "If this is what it takes,
then sure.
Let's do it."

58
MARIS

Maris is sweating
but she always feels most herself
this way
her body working hard to navigate
the unsteady terrain
of the woods on the outskirts of town,
heart pumping through
the steep climb
as they plunge deeper into the forest
and rise up amongst the tall trees.

"I haven't been out here yet,"
Genevieve says, not out of breath
at all
even though they have been on the move
for over an hour now
and Maris tosses her hair back
like she doesn't care that Genevieve is
in better shape.

Won't matter in the end,
will it?

⊰⟡⊱

She turns so she's walking backward
watching Genevieve below her.
"What, Coach didn't give you the
official tour
when you got here? And we have
so much to see!"
She gestures to the trees around them. "Look—

the woods! And—" She points somewhere
beyond Genevieve. "The town! Wow!"

"You make it sound like there's
nothing to do here," Genevieve says,
and she sounds so sincere and her face is so
serious
that it takes Maris a second to realize
Genevieve is joking.
When she does
she lets out a short laugh
without meaning to
catching herself too late
so that now Genevieve is the one
laughing
at her.

"Come on, you can find me funny,"
Genevieve says. "Isn't that the whole point?
Bonding, and shit?"

"I guess," Maris says, and turns
so her back is to Genevieve again.
Easier this way.
"I never said thanks."

"For what?"

"Not pressing charges,"
Maris says. "After
the fight. You could have."

"Like I said, I'm no
rat," Genevieve says. "Besides, I gave

as good as I got. No need to involve
the cops. I can be a bitch but
I'm not out to, like,
ruin a life like that."

"You think I have a life
to ruin?" Maris says.
"Nice." She meant it to sound
funnier
than it actually does.
*Come on, Genevieve, you can
find me funny!*

But Genevieve just says, "God, you
really have, like, no self-esteem,
don't you?"

⊰⊱

Maris stops,
flexes her fingers. "What?"

"You say it like you're nothing,"
Genevieve says. "Like you
have nothing at all, just because this town
is, yeah, a shithole, sure, but—
god, it's like you've
given up
before you've even gotten started."

"What do you know about it?"
Maris says. "You're not
from here. You live here now but
even with that—you live in one of the
nicest houses here. You don't have

to work. You didn't grow up
in this nothing town with no future—"

"There you go again," Genevieve says,
sounding almost amused. "You know
you're not, like, *bound* to this place. You could leave
if you wanted. Maybe you're not exactly destined
for college or whatever
but
that's only one way out.
You could pretty easily graduate and then
go be miserable
in some other place. Get a
job, an apartment you split
with some other miserable girl.
There *has* to be something else you want
from life
besides cheerleading. Or, shit,
if that's really it, I'm sure
there's some college out there
with a team that would take you.
Don't you *want* to believe
there's more than this?"

<<>>

Maris has spent months being
jealous
of Genevieve and Coach, but only now
does she see how alike they really are.
Everything Genevieve just said
could have come from Coach's lips
and it's jarring
to hear it
from the girl she has come to see as her

enemy. To know that Genevieve
just like Coach
thinks she could be more than she really is.

She knows they're wrong. They have to be
wrong, because if they were right
it would mean Maris would have to
try
and if she tried then she might fail, and
she'd rather not try at all than crash out
spectacularly
and have to come home
tail between her legs
new bruises, new scars.

Besides—
so what if Genevieve
suddenly has something
nice
to say to her? It's
too late. Maris can't go
soft
now. She can't let one conversation with Genevieve
distract her
from her *real* plan
her *real* goal
the one thing she knows she can do.

⊰⟷⊱

Maris starts moving again.
"Maybe there is something
more than this," she says, glancing over her shoulder
to make sure Genevieve is keeping pace.
They are almost to the ridge.

"I think about it," she says, and suddenly
the things she keeps secret from everybody else
in her life
are pouring out. "Everyone thinks I don't,
but I do think about the fact that
there's a whole big world out there. I don't want
my entire life to be
cheerleading
and this town
and nothing more than that. But I have
a mom who's, like, really sick, you know? And
I don't know if I could leave her
all by herself. And the things I want
feel so out of reach
like there's this huge fucking pit I don't know how to cross
because whatever it *would* take
would require me to become
a completely different person
than I am, and I can't do it. No matter
how much Coach asks me to
or how much Nell asks me to—"
Maris sighs.
"I don't want to be
a different person. I am
what I am.
I only wish
that was enough
for everybody else."

"Why are you telling me this?"
Genevieve asks, and
she is wary, looking back
the way they came
even as she keeps step with Maris.

What Maris thinks is:
I am telling you this
because I know
you'll never be able to tell anyone else
after I'm done with you.

But all Maris says is
"We're *bonding,*
aren't we?
Come on, Genevieve—"

—<—>—

It's a white flash of lightning
that stops Maris,
her mouth open as she looks up.

Around them the light is different,
has changed without Maris noticing.
They can barely see the sky
from deep inside the dense woods
but
Maris catches fragments of blackness
a twisting cloud
that clear spring day
vanished.

59

DOE

She watches the girls as they climb,
rivals on their way to
the top.

Exactly where Doe
needs them to be.

Now she ignores the insects crawling
over her flesh. So many years—
she has waited
so many years
for this, for what is
about to come to pass.

So long
that her own girls are rotten
and forgotten
now.

But soon
things will begin anew.

Doe watches the girls
and then she begins
to sing.

An old song
remembered at last. Sharp
discordant

a chord of crashing waves and shattering glass
threads twisted together
unstitching the sky
inviting the thunder, the
lightning.

60
MARIS

Genevieve looks from Maris
to the trees, swaying and bending beyond their normal bounds
in the wind that has picked up. "I think it's gonna—"
The sudden and suffocating rain
cuts Genevieve off
and in seconds they are soaked
down to their bones.

"Shit," Maris says, but it is lost
in the break of thunder right above them.
She's only wearing leggings,
a tank, a fleece,
thick gray socks inside her boots.
No one said anything about a storm.

⊰⊹⊱

No one said anything about a storm.
She thinks it again
as her teeth begin to knock together,
the shift from sweat to cold whiplash fast.
The rain is ice and
already it's washing rivulets of dirt and debris down the incline.

Maris looks at the water
streaming beneath her boots
and Genevieve, staring up into the storm,
hair plastered across her face.

Rain washes things away,
Maris thinks.

Things like footprints
and blood
and a person's true intent

right?

61
MARIS

Genevieve is looking
back the way they came,
the darkness of the woods ready
to swallow them up.
Maris knows what she's going to say
before she says it:

"We should head back!"
Genevieve has to raise her voice
over the wind.
"I don't think this is gonna pass
and
I don't want to
get stuck out here."

⊰⊹⊱

Maris pulls in a long breath
of stinging cold air,
the taste of soil on her tongue.

Around her the woods pulse
or maybe she imagines it.

They're so close to the ridge
if they just keep going—

⊰⊹⊱

Maris starts walking again. "No,"
she says, yells,
rain catching in her wide-open mouth.
"We should keep going!

There's a clearer path
on the other side of the ridge.
It'll be easier to—"

⊰⟷⊱

Her words get lost in the thunderclap
heavy above them
the vibration resonating low and sickening in Maris's belly
in her bones.

She looks over her shoulder
but the rain makes it so she can barely see
more than a foot in front of her.
"Genevieve—"

"Fuck this, Maris."
Genevieve's voice is a signal in the darkness.
"I'm going back right—"

⊰⟷⊱

There's a blinding
brilliant light
and Maris throws her hands up
to cover her eyes.

It feels like it lasts for an entire minute
although Maris knows that can't be right,
a jagged bolt from the sky,
striking too close.

"Jesus," she says,
the word instantly snatched away.
A singed dirt smell circles
and then the noise begins,

a chorus of groaning,
cracking,
and Maris looks up.

Sees the solid, towering tree that has been split in half
by the lightning
the scorched guts of it tearing open wider
and wider
yawning apart as one half stays standing to attention
and the other heads straight for the ground.

❮◄►❯

Another lightning flash
just enough to illuminate Genevieve
right there—

Maris watches it happen.
Watches the smoldering remains of the tree
ten times as tall as Genevieve, easy,
and thick like a steel beam
plummet toward her
the space where she was standing a split second before
empty now.

❮◄►❯

In the sudden quiet that follows
Maris stares at the still-standing remains of the tree.
If you saw it from the right angle,
she realizes,
you wouldn't know anything was wrong.
It's only from this side,
seeing the scarred bark and the
insides spilling out,
that you can see what happened.

In the sudden quiet
Maris presses her hands over her ears
wondering what happened to the wind, the rain.
It takes a second to register that
it's all still there
rain persistently pelting her skin.
The ringing in her head
is blocking the rest out, an echo
of the tree's collapse.

Maris drops her hands.
Wait.
Where the fuck is
Genevieve?

62
DOE

It is the most beautiful storm she
has ever called up.

Power coursing through her
once more, a feeling she thought
was no longer possible.

See the shock on the girls' faces
the reverence
as the lightning strikes
as the tree rends from the earth
crushing Genevieve beneath.

63
MARIS

Maris runs
falls and scrambles to her feet again
mud slicking her hands.
"No. No, no, no—"

When Maris reaches her she recoils.
Genevieve is crushed beneath the tree
and Maris is no expert
but she's pretty sure a human body
isn't built to take the hit
of a thousand pounds of wood and bark.
She's pretty sure a human body
isn't meant to look like that.

This was not how it was
supposed to happen.

Maris drops to her knees again,
by choice this time, crawling
across the silty broth that is the forest floor.
"Genevieve?" she says,
looking at her, lying there, eyes closed,
as still as the comatose girl
in a shitty fairy tale.

Is this it?
Maris wonders,
both shocked and
disappointed. *Is she*
dead

She digs her fingers into the dirt
clawing at the earth
like she might dig her way
to a version of reality
in which she didn't fuck up
yet again
have her moment of victory stolen
right out from under her.

"We were so close,"
Maris says
barely audible over the storm.
"The ridge is right up ahead. It was going to be
so easy. It was going to be
so perfect." A quick
crack to the skull
with a rock
and then Maris was going to send Genevieve
over the ridge and down
into the ravine
her pinballing the entire way
explaining away that fracture in her
skull.
Then she'd be dead
and out of Maris's way forever
except she couldn't even have that, couldn't even have
the chance to make things right
the way she wanted to.

Maris stares at Genevieve's
crushed form
and all the adrenaline
all the hate she'd been
so excited
to use when she picked up that rock
and brought it crashing down on Genevieve
is stuck inside, swirling
trapped.

And then Genevieve opens her eyes,
looks back,
unfocused.
"Maris," she manages, little more than a breathless gasp,
and then the rest is lost
in the thunder.

64
MARIS

She's not dead.
The relief that floods Maris is sharp.
Genevieve is not dead
yet.
It's not
all over.
There's still time.

Maris scrapes her hair out of her face
blinks off the rain
as she surveys Genevieve, lying
before her.

It's the angle of everything
that gives it away
how Genevieve's legs
seem like they want to take her
in the wrong direction
how her rib cage is splayed wide open under the tree
no longer protecting
her vital organs.

"Maris," Genevieve says once more
slow.
"Where— What happened?"

A giggle bubbles up
inside Maris
and she sits back on her heels
claps a hand over her mouth to keep it in.

What happened
Genevieve
is that I brought you out here
to
kill
you.
And then lightning brought this tree down
right on top of you
and I thought you were dead, and my chance to hurt you
was gone.
But you're still alive
and I am going to wait with you here
until you're not.
I am going to watch you die
Genevieve
and I
am going
to enjoy every second.

"The storm brought a tree down."
Maris has to raise her voice
so that Genevieve can hear, but she still sounds
unnervingly clear
calm.
"It crushed you. But I probably don't need
to tell *you* that."

Genevieve blinks
her mouth opening slowly, a few words
all she can seem to manage.
"Go . . . get . . . help."

Look at her.
Maris can see the effort

each word, each
ragged breath takes,
the smallest trickle of blood leaking
from the corner of Genevieve's mouth.
She's alive right now
but she doesn't have long.
And maybe, maybe
if Maris called right now
help might be able to come save her.

Maris eases off her knees
sits on the forest floor, legs folded in front of her
the perfect angle
from which to watch.

"I can't do that,"
Maris says. "That's not how
this is going to end. You don't get to
survive this.
You were never going to.
Don't worry.
I don't think it's going to take long at all.
Let's just wait it out
together."

Genevieve lets out a
keening
sound, and for a moment it seems like
she's trying to move, straining with all
her might,
but all her effort does
is turn her cry into a guttural moan
and it is some time
before she can speak, before she says,

"Why—are you—doing
this
to me?"
A rasping breath, and then, "Call
somebody. Find
someone.
Please."

⊰⊱

Maris gets to her feet
and moves closer to Genevieve
up against the tree pinning her down.
She runs her fingers across the bark
and inhales,
the still-burning air
the smoldering wood
the ice on the wind.

She stands on tiptoes
and peers over the fallen tree.
From this angle
she can see how the bone at the top of Genevieve's thigh
has torn clean through her flesh
snapped right in half.
Bends down
and reaches to touch
where the wood
meets Genevieve
everything slick and red.
She can see how Genevieve's insides
are outside now,
glistening pink.

⊰⊱

"Everything was good
before you came along."
Maris looks down at Genevieve
staring up at her so helplessly
pathetic.
"Well. Not everything, but
I had the team, and I had Coach. And then
you showed up.
I just want things back to
how they were, and I finally realized
that was never going to happen
with you around. I got the team back, but
you were still going to be there, and I
couldn't have that. I needed to
get rid
of you.
I had a whole plan, you know?"
She sighs. "Sucks
that I didn't get to do it myself, but
if this is what I'm left with, then I'll
gladly
sit here and watch you
die."
She shrugs, even as she watches
Genevieve's face contort
in horror.
"At least this way, I can be telling the truth
when I say
it was
a horrible, horrible
accident."

65

GENEVIEVE

She is swallowing blood
and realizing
all too late
that she has underestimated Maris
and how far she was willing to go
what she was willing to do—

Genevieve stares up
as the world flashes white
and says the only thing she can think of
a waste of words because she knows there is
no way out
of this—

"I don't want to die."

66
MARIS

The sky is full dark now.
Hours have passed
hours Maris has spent counting
the stretches between Genevieve's breaths
never looking away
from Genevieve's broken body
watching her face slacken
her eyes roll beneath tissue-thin lids

and finally Maris hears the rattle
of another breath, and counts,
and she gets to twenty, thirty,
an entire minute
and nothing more comes.

Moves to her
waves her hand in front of glassy eyes
and she is gone
Maris understands.
She watched all the life
drain slowly
so
slowly
out of Genevieve
and now all that is left
is her corpse
for real this time.

She waits to see
if guilt will come, if
shame, remorse,

will flood her, but
instead it feels like
something has opened up inside her
and she can do nothing but
laugh
until there are tears streaming down her face
until her stomach hurts from it all.

When her laugh finally fades
Maris looks around her
and realizes it's time to
pull herself together.
She only gets away with this
if everyone is convinced by her performance
and so she rehearses it in her head, what
she'll say
when she makes the phone call. *Please
please we need help, we were hiking when
the storm hit
and a tree—the lightning—please she's hurt
bad, we need help
right now, please please please—*

But when she takes out her phone
of course there's no service.
"Shit," Maris says, and looks at her hands
dark with dirt
or with Genevieve's blood
she can't tell.

"I'm going to get help,"
she announces—
just to be safe, just

in case
there is anyone hiding out there
who will be called on later
to verify Maris's story.

"I'll come right back,"
she says loudly. "Okay,
Genevieve? I'll be back
with help
as fast as I can."

⪻⪼

She keeps moving forward
the light from her phone her only guide,
an uneasiness building—
she had been so focused
on watching Genevieve die
that she let the storm recede in her mind
but the rain is still lashing
the sky intermittently flashing white
the rumble of thunder coming after.

She has to move forward
because the route they came up
is flooded out now

and besides
she wasn't wrong earlier—
the ridge was close
and now she's there
where the trees begin to thin
and Maris can faintly see the lights of town in the distance,
the near-black sky surrounding her.

She stumbles
can feel the woods watching her
as she steadies herself and keeps moving
mud sucking at her boots
rain pounding her skin
breaths coming deep

stumbles again
tries to regain her balance but fails
and pitches forward
hands thrown out to break her fall—

She lands
on her hands and knees
in the ooze of the forest floor
and her stomach flips
reacting a half second late, even as Maris tells herself
she's fine, there's no reason to be
afraid. As she
laughs a little
at her own clumsiness
so silly, silly girl.

But as she climbs up out of the muck
she still feels unsteady
as if the ground is shifting beneath her feet—

Shit.

Maris looks down
in time to see the ground give way

and she falls.

67

TEAM

When we woke up on Saturday
heads woolly and mouths desert dry
we thought it must be early,
we cursed the world for waking us up
in the still-small hours of the morning
when the sky was that dark.

But we checked our phones and saw it was late,
beyond midday,
and we peeled our blinds up and stared at the blackening sky
the roll of cloud and pressure.

⸙

Then the warnings came through on our phones:
extreme weather
they said, and
risk of flooding
and
risk of falling trees
and
possibility of life-threatening situations
and—

⸙

There was something exciting about it,
something loud about the air
and the anticipation, waiting
for the sky to split open
and the rain to come.

Our messages swarmed

us in our bedrooms with the doors locked
keeping out siblings and stepparents and fights
keeping out silence and cold.
It's not often that we had those moments,
the kind other people romanticize,
rain on the window and you
curled up inside,
warm light keeping you company.

⤝⤞

my head is killing me

why did we think tequila was a good idea

does anyone have my shoes? I can't find my shoes

oh my god I'm gonna throw up again

if I don't get hash browns soon I'm DEF gonna throw up

don't talk about hash browns

what time did we even get home?

I woke the baby up when I came in, I'm gonna pay for that shit

claire did I see you get that hot girl's number

claire you dirty little slut

proud of u claire

lol yeah but I'm not gonna use it

did you see how old she was? like at LEAST 25

ew no

maris ur being quiet!!!

she's prob still drunk

felt so GOOD to be OUT!! and now we are BACK

now everything can go back to the way it was before

except for genevieve

well yeah but who cares about her

I'm so over her

it's just about us now

back to the way it always was

Outside the old trees
creaked and snapped
against the sky dark, almost purple, like a week-old bruise
the kind you get when a basket toss goes wrong
and you take a knee to the face.

We ignored the homework we had
the thought that after showing how
good
we could be
that our teachers would be expecting it
(they should know better).

Instead we slept it all off
and promised ourselves
we'd stretch tomorrow.

❈

Later, when the hangovers were gone
and we were zoned out on cartoons
and painting our toes
and idly watching porn
and examining the pores on our noses in the mirror—

Later, when we were
pressed up to the windowpane
watching the sky streak
and the rain lash
(we like that word, that description,
the water like a punishment all its own)—

Later, when we were sinking
into the comfort of having clawed our way back—
that was when Nell's message came.

⪡⟶⪢

Have any of you heard
from Maris?

68
TEAM

Middle of the night
we lie in our beds,
sinking into sleep to the sound of the storm.

Haven't heard from her since last night,
Nell said.
She's not with you?

⊰⊱

We don't worry about Maris.
She's our leader,
fearless,
but there was something in Nell's words—

⊰⊱

Storm rages on outside.
We are safe, asleep,
a dream—

Water over our mouths so that we can't breathe
and a dark girlshape space
and a crooning phrase repeated
over and over into our chests,
the woods the woods the woods the woods the woods—

⊰⊱

When we wake
before the sun is up
it is with a warm sheen on our skin,
sweat like we're in the gym,

but we are still here in our beds
and Maris is—

⤙⤚

In the woods.
We remember.
We know it.

69

TEAM

Prairie is the first to say something.
We are all together
at the old playground early Sunday morning,
dawn still off in the distance,
us sheltering under the rusted remains of the jungle gym.
The storm has lessened now,
calmed some.
The news showed trees ripped out by their roots
and houses with roofs bowing inward
and floods over the low roads
but *no injuries reported,*
the white brunette with the dazzling teeth said.

We know, though,
how unlikely that is to be true.
Not with Maris out in the woods,
for whatever fucking reason
she decided that was a good idea,
because how long has she been out there?
If no one's heard from her since Friday night?

(We don't question
how it is we know where she is
how it is we all dreamed the same thing—
there is no time
not while Maris is still missing.)

So it's Prairie who speaks,
Prairie who says,
"We have to go get her.
We have to find her."

-‹-‡-›-

And it's August who doesn't say
what if there's nothing to find?

70

TEAM

We head out
toward the woods
slowing through the surface water
that slips across the roads
and asking each other
why Maris would have gone
to the woods
at all?

And did she even go home
on Friday night?

And should we have noticed
there was something wrong?

Because that's what
we all keep thinking, that
she went out there
to do the worst thing,
the thing we all throw around too casually
I have to work a double shift Jesus I'm gonna kill myself
but in all sincerity promise each other we wouldn't do,
a no-suicide pact.

Why else would she be out there?

⤙⤚

Us in our chain
of shitty cars,
cars paid for with
those mall nights

and odd jobs
rewarded with cash.

Driving through our shitty town
where nobody respects us
but it's okay,
because we have each other.

That is what Maris has taught us,
but now we're all wondering
if it was bullshit
and if she can't believe
then how do we?

<<->>

It's August who gets the call.
Coach's name on the screen.

Coach never calls.
We have her number
for emergencies,
for reminders,
always in text form.

But Coach calling?

Prairie, driving, grips the wheel,
knuckles white.

August answers
and we hold our breath.

<<->>

"Coach?"
August sounds scared,
we hear it,
even though she's trying to hide it.
"Is everything okay?"

August puts it on speaker,
so we can hear
when Coach says,
"Sorry to be calling so early but—
do any of you
have any idea
where Genevieve is?"

<-<->->

Genevieve?

Fuck.

71

TEAM

Coach sounds edgy,
nervous,
the same way we all feel
in this moment.

"Her mom is concerned
and frankly, so am I.
Genevieve went out yesterday around noon
and never came home.
We're just trying to make sure
we cover all our bases
before we start to . . ."

We don't know what the end of that sentence is,
worry or *panic* or *file a missing person report,*
but we do know,

looking at each other,
we know
this cannot be a coincidence.

⸻⟡⸻

On the other end of the line
Coach is waiting, and Prairie pinches the skin
on the inside of August's elbow.

"Oh," August says, trying for
gentle concern. "No, I don't think
we've seen her. Well—
I haven't. But I'll check
with the girls. And I'll let you know.

I'm sure
she's fine, you know?"

"Yeah," Coach says,
but she sounds distracted.
"Okay, well. Let me know
what the girls say."

August curls her hands into fists,
bones inside her fingers cracking.
Hang up, hang up, hang up.

But then Coach speaks again,
an afterthought, almost:
"I tried Maris first,
but she didn't answer." Coach
pauses.
"August?
Are you there?"

72
TEAM

When we get to the parking area at the edge of the woods
Nell is there.

We abandon our cars
and cross the gravel
to meet her.
She's waiting with hiking boots
and a waterproof jacket
and a flashlight in hand.

Of course, Nell is prepared
and here we are
in sneakers
and leggings
and chewed-cuff sweatshirts.

But Nell says nothing about our attire,
just looks at us like she always does,
wary and worn out.

She doesn't like us
and we don't like her
but Maris is our common ground,
our girl,
so here we all are, because we couldn't not tell her
what we knew.
We couldn't not say to her
that wherever Maris is inside those woods
we're pretty sure Genevieve is there, too.

⊰⊹⊱

There's that look again, Nell's
wary face, like we might be
making this all up, like we
are playing some kind of prank.
"But . . . why the fuck would they be together? Maris
hates Genevieve. What is going on here? What
aren't you saying?"

We know she won't believe us
if we say
we have the same questions as you.
We don't know how we know Maris is here,
we just do. And we don't know why Maris
would have brought Genevieve here.
Especially not after we just got our right to cheer back.

And anyway—who's to say
that Maris was the one in charge? Maybe
it's Gen's fault
that they're out here, that they've
been out here.

"Whatever,"
Nell says when we don't answer her. "Whatever."
And throws another flashlight
to August, and says,
"What are you waiting for?"

⹊⟡⹉

We stay together,
snaking through the trees,
slipping on the swampy ground
as dawn breaks.

The rain is still freezing
and stings our open mouths as we call out for Maris
following a path we hope she took
having exactly zero real idea.

But we follow Nell,
up ahead,
August right behind her.

Nell calls Maris's name the loudest
calling over the rain, the trees still moving,
shush-shush-shush of foliage.

❖

We don't want to call for Genevieve.

But we do it anyway.

73

TEAM

They're okay
they're okay
we're going to find them both perfectly okay

that thought thrums beneath our voices
as we call their names
into the darkness before us.

⊰⊱

Mud cakes our sneakers,
flecks our legs
and Claire's arms
where she stumbled and fell.

We don't know how long we have been walking
don't know whether we are getting closer to Maris
or further away
but we keep working our way through the woods,
digging into the earth to climb,
still calling calling calling

and Nell tells us to watch the ground
watch out for a sign,
a shoe print
or
snagged piece of clothing
or
lost earring.

⊰⊱

"Like some Hansel and Gretel shit,"
August says,
loud like she doesn't care
if Nell hears her.
We ignore her
and press on
but August keeps going:
"She really thinks
it could be that easy? Does she even—"

⤝⤞

We look back,
see August down on hands and knees,
and we call to Nell and Prairie to slow down,
stop,
while we pick her back up

except when we reach for her
August bats us away
and we follow her gaze
to what she is staring at,
what she tripped on.

"Whoa," Prairie says,
and she kicks at the out-of-place branches
that tripped August,
the top of a tree
somehow down on the ground with us.
When we look we see
charred insides, as if someone took a blowtorch
and burned it right in two.

Nell squats to run her fingers along the bark
lifting her hand to her nose after.

"I think
lightning brought it down,"
she says, as if she's the expert.

August pulls herself up
sniffs the air.
"Yeah," she says. "You
smell that? Like
burning."

Nell is walking along the length of the fallen tree now.
"I've never seen this before.
It's almost like . . ."

We shiver in the cutting wind
waiting, waiting.
When Nell doesn't speak
for too long
August calls out to her
her voice high, strained. "What, Nell?
What is it?"

Nell looks back at us
a shaking hand pointing at the ground.

"I found Genevieve."

74

TEAM

We move, our feet
sticking in the mud
as we make our way to Nell
and to—

Genevieve.
Pinned beneath the tree carcass
and we've never seen a dead body like this before
but it's so obvious we don't even bother
with the *is she?* and the *Genevieve, hey, Gen, look at us—*

⪪⪫

Her eyes are two black holes
slack jaw
unnerving stillness even as the forest lives, breathes
around her.

Blood on her fingers
and dirt matted in her hair

cold blue sheen
to her skin

and we have the words on our tongues
but don't say them

don't say anything

just stare at her limp crushed body
and listen to the sound

of Nell emptying her stomach
behind us.

❖

We don't say anything
just stand there,
the loudest sound rain hitting,
and let the fear we usually keep so far at bay
flood our bones.

Genevieve is dead.
But we still don't have Maris
so where is she?

What has the storm
done to her?

75

DOE

Yes
it's a deviation from the old song
but not a deviation from the plan. This was always
how Doe wanted it to go.
Genevieve
was never the vessel
only the
necessary sacrifice. Couldn't
burn her
as she had the Mayweather boy
because then where would the blood come from?
Doe learned from her girls
all those years ago
that blood must be spilled
for the magic to work.
And for big magic
she reasons
no finger prick will do.
No: For what she desires
only death would be
sacrifice enough.
Enough for Doe to be able
to reshape her bindings
to stitch herself into the skin
of the one she truly wants:

Maris.

"Maris!"

We are hoarse,
tired from screaming her name
our hope fading.

We try to understand
what happened here.
Genevieve is dead, a casualty
of the storm,
but what about Maris? Is she
a casualty somewhere, too? Was she
with Genevieve
when that fallen tree crushed her?

"Maris!"

She must have gone to get help,
we think.
If she and Genevieve were together
when Genevieve got hurt
then Maris would have called someone
maybe run for someone,
wouldn't she.

⊰⊱

   "Would she?"
       "She wouldn't just, like, leave her here to die, right?"
                 "Well. Maris
                 hates Genevieve."
"But that's, like, really fucked up. That she might do that."

"Are you saying Maris is fucked up? Are you saying
you're *not* fucked up?"

"Watch it, Prairie."

"No, I'm just saying—"

"She wouldn't. Not after all that work we
did. To be good. To get the team back."

"August's right. So she hates Genevieve. I don't like her either,
but—shit."

"Maris wouldn't just leave her here. She's a bitch
but she's not stupid."

"If she did that—it would fuck everything up, beyond belief. Not
just us, but her life. For real."

"She wouldn't do it."

"Okay, so then—where the fuck did she go?"

Where is she?

-‹-›-

Bone tired and cold
to our marrow
we keep searching.

"Maris!"

Trying not to think about
the way Genevieve's eyes stared
right through us.

Trying not to think about how
unlike most of us
she has parents who are going to
shatter
when they find out she's gone.

She has Coach
who missed her enough
to call us for help.

Maris's mom didn't pick up our calls at first
and eventually answered just to say,
"I'm sure she's fine," in a tiny, wavering voice
like she was saying it only
to try to convince us, convince
herself. "Will you call me
when you find her?"
And we said sure, of course,
knowing that it was the most she
could offer
that even when her daughter was missing
she couldn't rise to the occasion.
Sad, we thought
pretending some of us didn't know all too well
what Celia Larsen is like
pretending we all weren't wondering
if our moms would be any better
some of us wishing
we still had a mom around at all.

❖

"*Maris!*"

What little light there is
strains to reach us through the canopy
and *she won't last another night*
we think.

"*Maris!*"

—‹•›—

The wind dies, finally,
and that is when
we hear it.
A scream
carrying through the trees.

77

MARIS

There's something in her airway
making it hard to breathe.

Her brain registers this
the moment before Maris
comes to,
and it is nothing but
animal instinct
that makes her turn her head and
retch.

The dark sky above glitches in
and
out
and Maris—

⪡⪢

The next time she comes to
it is with a noise
of shock.

Staring up at the gray cloud
Maris isn't sure where she is
when she is
only that her body
feels both on fire
and glacier numb.

When she flicks her tongue out
she tastes iron,
blood crusted onto her lips.

Remember,
she tells herself,
a command
like she gives the girls in practice—

Yes. Practice. Cheer.
I cheer. We have a team, my name is
Maris,
and I . . .

Think.
Remember.

I was walking.
In the woods?
Yes, in the woods, because—
Fuck.
Genevieve.

Genevieve is dead.
The memory comes with a
warmth, a
joy
at the knowledge that the girl who plagued her
has finally fallen.
But
then what?

Then I was . . .
walking through the woods
and the rain never stopped—

She remembers then
looking up at the sky

like she is now
but one moment there was solid ground beneath her feet
and the next
nothing.

She remembers
dropping through the air
hands grasping at emptiness
and that's all.

⊰⊶⊷⊰

The moon is nowhere to be seen
hidden behind the rain,
Maris thinks.
Or wait—is it
the sun she should be looking for?

It is moments or minutes or hours later
she can't tell.
Has been trying to move herself
but though her brain says
feet, flex
and
hands, hold
they don't play along
and is it because she is so frozen
or is it the bones broken inside of her
that keep her bolted to the ground?

⊰⊶⊷⊰

And then—
the touch of something
against her cheek.

Eyes flicker open once more
her brain catching up
a minute behind—

Someone is here.
Somebody has found me.

She looks to her savior
and her gaze meets eyes pure white
in the face not of a human
but an animal—

a deer—

⌐⟨⟩⌐

Maris inhales hard
a sharp pain splintering through
her ribs.

And then a flood of relief
because this creature standing over her,
rotted-out flesh
coat glossy onyx where
it still grows,
Maris knows it. She's seen it before—

many times, it is
rushing back now
filling her mind
and she's never been good at remembering
her dreams
but she remembers this deer.

So this is a dream,
she thinks, ready to
weep.
So I am dreaming
and I'm going to be okay
really.

⊰⊹⊱

The creature walks around Maris, *tick-tick-tick*
of its hooves in the dirt.
She watches it from below
gazing up at this thing towering over her
has the impression of the belly of a ruined church
its shining ribs that appear and disappear beneath inky skin
like rafters holding up a spire.

"How long,"
Maris manages,
the crust on her lips flaking
falling into her mouth.
"How long before I wake up?"

The creature turns its ivory gaze on her
and a whisper vibrates somewhere
deep
in her mind—

Wake up?
Oh, Maris. You're not dreaming.
You're dying.

78

DOE

Dying, not dreaming,
Doe knows.
She's not completely dead yet
but Doe had to wait
pass the hours watching Maris get weaker and weaker
(the same way Maris had watched Genevieve die, Doe thinks, so
poetic)
so there would be
no chance
of Maris fighting back
of Maris getting up and fleeing.

Look at her.
Even in so much pain she is still strong, still
trying.
Look at her—
writhing in the dirt
as if she can escape the *dream*
that way—
look at her fighting the truth
even when she knows it's no use.

On the air
Doe can hear the team's voices carry from far away
coming for their girl
in the early dawn light
as Doe's girls
ran after her in that lightning night.

Doe thinks of Iris
the one who knew what she was as soon as she set eyes

on the ink-black little creature.
And Bonnie
the one who had named her
the one whose blood
flows through Maris.

Bonnie would understand,
Doe thinks. She would know
why Doe needs to do this, why
it had to be Maris, why
she cannot bear another moment
trapped in this body
even if it means
dooming Maris to a life
inside the body of
a wretched decaying deer.

Doe was born with a power
that blurs the question: Are you
god
or are you
monster?

Finally
with this act
she intends to find out.

79

MARIS

Maris thrashes against the earth
gasping with the pain of it
but she can't stay still
can't stay asleep
has to wake up wake up wake up—

You know that's not going to happen.

That whisper in her head again
and Maris pretends she can't hear it
pretends it isn't there

except, like before,
she knows she's heard it already.
A familiar sound
winding its way around her mind.
The voice of this creature.

She digs her hands into the dirt.
But how the *fuck*—

"Dreams," she says aloud, like that
will reassure her. "Weird shit happens
in dreams."

And in life.
You should know that
better than most. You, sleepwalking through the night—
remember? That's how
we first met.

Maris swallows. "I don't sleepwalk."
But—

Her eyes close
blackness where the creature used to be.
And she remembers
waking up with muddied sheets
scrubbing the stains out in the bathroom
and windows she could have sworn she'd locked before bed
swinging wide open
and coming to in Nell's kitchen
and all these half-forgotten dreams
that she locked away
too tired to figure them out.

Her eyes snap open
and the creature is staring down at her
and Maris can't look away, this time,
from those empty eyes.

"I was sleepwalking.
I was out in the night
and that's where we met—"
Crossroads, she remembers, she can see the first time:
her in a white dress, this *thing*
in the middle of the road like a statue.
"I was sleepwalking
not dreaming
and this isn't a dream—"

The deer creature
tilts its head.

No, it's not a dream. I wish it could be
because despite everything
I do admire you, Maris, and
I don't want to cause you
pain.
It's only that
this is the way it had to be.
I needed you
to help me get here. I needed you to believe that this
was all your plan. I needed you to bring Genevieve
out here, so I could—

"Genevieve."
Maris breathes her name
and everything
comes rushing at her
comes clear in her mind:

Nights spent wandering town
talking to this—this—this
thing, this monster, a warped version of
a deer. Telling it
all about how she hated Genevieve, and then
it told her how it wanted to help, how
it could help her get rid of Genevieve.
Bring her out to the woods, it said. *We'll*
take care of her.
Make it look like
an accident.
Then you won't have
to worry about her anymore.
It's the only way
to fix things.

And when Maris had said she wasn't
sure, didn't
know if she could really
kill Genevieve
and convince everyone afterward
that she was innocent,
the creature had said
I believe in you. Trust me. Everything
will go according to plan.

Maris had woken up
and forgotten the creature
but the idea stayed
growing like a sapling in her mind
convincing her it was all her own idea. That it was
a *good* idea.

Tears slip
from the corners of her eyes
down her face and into the earth.
"You
lied to me. You
used me. I never did
anything to you, I—"
She drags in a breath. "Why did you kill her?
Why didn't you let me do it?
Why are you
killing *me*?"

You brought her out here.
That was all I needed from you.
I had to be the one who killed her because I was the one who needed
an offering. The magic requires a sacrifice, so that is what I gave it.
As for you—

The creature comes closer
lowers its head to press its nose
to her forehead, and Maris
makes a noise somewhere between
a cry of pain and a cry of fear
its skin so cold against hers.

You aren't going to die. Not yet, at least. You will live—your
spirit, soul, whatever it is you want to call all the ineffable things that
make you
you.
But not in this body. In mine.
And I will take yours
so that I can live.
A long, long time ago
a girl who looked a lot like you
locked me away. Tied me up
so I couldn't be seen, and even though she restrained me I
grew to love her. All of them. But then they left me, and I
knew of no way out of those bindings, until I met you. We
share something, you and I, a connection
made in the past, with an offering of the highest kind. We were
already fated
and who am I to interfere
with fate?

Maris can't make sense of any of it—
what girl
what offering
what connection
—but one thing
she understands.
Fated.

She always knew
she was going to die in this town.

The creature's tongue flicks out
to taste her tears.

I wish
what I am about to do to you
could be sweeter
but I got tired of being sweet
such a long time ago.

And then the creature begins to sing.

⊰⊱

It is a slow, slinking song
that wraps around Maris's bones
and she is lulled, for a moment,
cradled in the comfort of the deer's
beautiful strange voice

and then, so suddenly, so forcefully, so
unbelievably violently
Maris is
torn in half.
The feeling of herself
cleaving from her own body,
a knife scraping everything that animates her
from the frame of her being—
it is a pain unlike anything else
that lullaby turned into a thousand razor slices.

Maris cries out

a scream of everything she has left.
Feels the rasp of regret against the
soft flesh of her throat,
a violent noise that carries
on the quiet wind
as if the storm has ceased, only for now,
only for her.

The creature sings louder
white eyes glowing golden now—
and in the distance, Maris sees another golden glow
like the fireflies she saw at the lake, years ago,
her and her mom camping in a tiny tent—

But no, she half remembers,
finding the truth
amongst misty memories.
That was a story she read
and imagined could be hers.
She has never seen
fireflies.

⋖⟷⋗

—Maris watches
time unfurl backward:

Genevieve bleeding

the determined march of their hiking boots
step-step-step out of time

herself in the night
hanging bejeweled chains on the creature's antlers
nodding at instructions whispered

the creature healing backward, becoming whole, skin
knitting back together, becoming
supple and shiny

a pile of ravaged bodies, dull fire-damaged faces

those same faces coming alive,
running through wildflower fields
screaming delight anger adulation

hot summer rain

hands reaching for, cradling, worshipping
an ink-black fawn.

80

DOE

It's a different sound,
this time,
Doe's song.
A new tune
for a new use of her powers.
Cool and piercing
a tone that contorts Maris's face.

She sings
like she used to so often
and the odd melodies wrap around the girl on the ground
travel back and snake around Doe's own body
slipping between her ribs
around the emptiness of her throat
burning a course through her remnant flesh.

It is working
Doe realizes
and a sharp joy ignites—

It is working, this
idea, half memory and half
wish
that the ties that bind them together
could allow Doe
to slip inside this girl
for the girl to take her place
inside the deer's body.

She sings but
instead of calling raindrops to fall from the air

or petals to unfurl
she calls to the cells in Maris's blood, to the
marrow in her bones. She calls
to herself, the
memories and heart and mind and
very essence of herself
and rejoices
as freedom calls.

81
MARIS

Maris has always been reckless,
the razors and the burns and the speeding down dark roads,
the body pushed to the point of breakdown,
the love for a girl who was bound to leave her,
and she did it all because she didn't care,
she thought,
what was she anyway but a dead-end girl
but now she's about to be a dead girl and only now
now does she want to live

only now does she want to run
into her mother's arms, tell her
it's okay, that she loves her, that
she knows
her mom loves her too
as best she can

only now does she realize
she's never going to have the chance
to say that to her mom
to say anything to her ever again

like she'll never be able to tell August
that she's sorry for the way she
treated her
toyed with her
and she'll never be able to tell the team that
they hold Maris together
more than they could have ever known

never be able to show Coach
how much better she really can be
or prove to Nell
that she isn't a lost cause
surprise everyone by finding her way
figuring her shit out—

but there will be no apartment of her own
no high ceilings or tall windows
no fantasy becoming real
no life outside of West Eaton

no life

⫷⫸

and she is a cliché, a
coward, she knows, but
with what little there is left of her
she makes promises,
as if that will fix the pain
of realizing all she had to lose
only now, only once it has become
too late

I will not kiss August and
I will not hate my mother and
I will not cut myself and
I will let Nell leave this place and
I will be good, for real, forever, just
give me back my body
give back my body
give back

82

DOE

Then comes—

the painful wrench
memory lifting, shearing away
from flesh
and Doe is weightless.

Halfway between
she watches a story
play out on the air:

A girl made of anger and sadness and a thirst for power
a girl who knows she is worshipped, adored, but
for whom that adoration isn't enough. A girl who can't see
what is right in front of her
who sleepwalked into her own
ending.

Halfway between
and the song is almost done.

Doe watches another story:
Bonnie, living and dying so young
and the act of vengeance Doe carried out
on her behalf.

And then this girl
sent like another offering
payment for what Doe did

a reward, perhaps, for
all she gave.

Doe hears voices on the wind
again:
the team
closer now.

She can feel their love
the adoration
soon to be Doe's to
claim, to
bathe in.

She will be more careful this time,
she promises herself. She won't
forget what a life without worship
is, she won't
be so reckless this time, put the team
in danger like she did
Bonnie
and Iris
and the others.

She will not become complacent
will not take the team's love for granted
the way Maris has.

And she will never let herself forget
what it took to get here.
She will remember
her girls and their violent end,

Genevieve and Maris
and the sacrifice they became.

Halfway between
and the song ends .
melody echoing
on the last of the storm wind.

I will be good
stop
let me
not going to
but I don't want
Nell
want to live
please
Mom
this will
please

84

TEAM

We crash through the trees
no longer bothering to take care
because the more measured our steps
the longer it will take us
to reach her.

We keep on calling
but Maris doesn't call back
and in the back of our minds
the thought, the worry,
that we willed ourselves to hear a voice
that wasn't really there.

Then Nell stops,
throws a hand out
halting us,
holding us—

"This way."

⃪⃖⃗⃕

We have to trust Nell, have to
follow her down down down
across slick forest floor
and we keep calling.
Think of all the times we have yelled
Maris's name before, out
the windows of our cars
and in dirty smoky bars
and as she flew across the floor
her body a twisting blur.

Now we call
hoping our voices
aren't crying out for a dead girl
hoping she is still a part of us
because yes, we want her to live, but also because,
selfish and cowardly,
we don't know who we will be
without her.

So we are rushing, and the earth beneath is
soft and unsteady, but we ignore that
until Claire screams,
short and sharp and surprised,
and we whip around as one
to see her beginning to fall—

⊰⊷⊱

For a second Claire hovers
the knife edge between safe and not,
and we think we are about to lose another one—

But August is closest,
reaches out to catch Claire's hand,
an instinctual grab,
and then Prairie grabs on to August,
and more hands reach for Prairie,
and we all pull
and Claire trips back up
onto solid ground.

It was only a second
but Claire collapses, hands and knees,
panting

as we watch her and wipe the rain
from our eyes.

And we are about to say
get up, let's go
when Nell points down, beyond the edge
where Claire was headed, and says
"Oh, *shit*."

❖

Beneath us
there she is
another girl
lying still in the clearing
like a small broken doll.

Maris.

Found, at last.

85

TEAM

When we reach her
she is so still
and washed out, all the richness
in her skin bleached out
by the storm, the cold.
Her left leg bent in a way
it shouldn't be
and her clothes stained with
a dark rust red
we know is blood.

<‑+‑>

"Someone call
911."

August kneels at Maris's side,
reaches out—

"No!" Nell says. "Don't
touch her. Don't
move her. We don't know
how hurt she is—"

August looks up, hand
still reaching. We need to know she's alive,
and August puts two fingers
on the inside of Maris's wrist—

We can't stand how cold she looks
start ripping off our jackets and sweatshirts
surrounding Maris so we can lay them

feather soft on top of her,
because we can't do nothing—

One of us holds her phone
to her ear, speaking in breathy tones: "Our friend,
she's hurt, and she's been out
all night
in the storm,
please send somebody—"

And then Nell says "Maris!"
in a way so intimate we feel suddenly like we are
intruding—

But we look at her anyway
and Maris has opened her eyes,
and she's staring up like she doesn't see us,
and it must be the catch
of a flashlight beam on her face
that is giving her eyes this odd golden glow,
and then she blinks,
and exhales, one long sigh,
and says
"I'm alive."

BEGIN ANEW

I'm alive.
Doe thinks it,
revels in it,
as a pain worse than she has ever known tears through her.

But she is euphoric, she is
ecstatic
to finally feel so much, to be
alive alive alive—

"I'm alive."
And Doe realizes she has said it aloud
and she has *spoken*
the working of lips, rolling tongue
two rows of blunt teeth pressing against
the wetness of mouth

It worked.
It worked, she thinks
an overwhelming awe
pushing everything else into the background
because somehow her plan
her magic
the whispers she fed Maris
the years of longing to be alive, to be seen, to be *real*
came together perfectly and
look, she has a *body* now!
Look at her skin, taut and whole! Her
bones! Hidden and no longer home to vile maggots
but protecting her delicate organs beneath
her heart that beats

her lungs that swell and deflate
like flowers blooming in the sun
and closing under moonlight.
She did this
with her song
the sacrifice
the belief that she could wield the same kind of magic
that her girls had first shown her
all those years ago.

Sacrifice.
The memory of it
brings Doe a little sorrow
a harmony to awe's melody.
She doesn't take sacrifice lightly.
Genevieve—
well. It is unfortunate
that she arrived when she did, fit
the plan so neatly.
And Maris—she was not worthless
and she could have done so much more with her life
her body
it's just that—

Doe needed it more.

Lying there on the forest floor
Doe can feel that body:
the tightness of muscle wrapped around bone
blood rushing through veins
the slick chill of cold earth beneath the body.

My body, now.

Eyes open
and Doe has never seen so clear.
Everything golden
a crowd of sirens watching over her—
the team, Maris's girls.

My girls, now.

It's almost too much
all those eyes on her
to be seen, to be
so seen
after all this time.

And then the one with dark hair feline eyes
the one Maris loved—
Nell, Doe knows—
takes her hand
and wraps it around the hand
that used to belong to Maris
and now belongs to Doe.

It has been so long
since Doe has been truly touched
and she feels good enough to laugh
so good it erases the pain radiating through her broken body.

"Don't worry,"
Nell says, and she is
relieved,
Doe hears,
gazes around at the girls and sees
they are all so relieved

to find their leader here
alive.

Doe tries the mouth again, words coming out
low and clean.
"The storm," she says. "The storm—"
The storm was perfect.
Nell squeezes her hand again.
"Don't worry,"
she repeats. "It's going to be okay.
It's all going to be okay."

Doe sinks into her body at those words.
Her *body*, her new home, new world, with a thousand
new chances
ready for her to take.
A thousand new possibilities—
because now that she has done this once,
now that she has shed that rotten old vessel,
she can see the truth of herself laid bare.
The power, the magic
that is everything she is, and she has
brought it all with her
stitched it all into this new body
to have and to hold.

My body, Doe thinks again
takes a deep, shocking breath
luxuriating in the sore rise and fall
of her rib cage, her chest.

There is a sudden roaring rush, like
an unseen river breaking its banks

or the sizzle and snap of electricity, fingers plugged
directly into a socket.
Takes her a moment to understand
that the noise is not out there but inside of her—
power, fully unbound and flooding every inch of her body.

My body, she thinks again, the stretch of a smile, the
thrill of it all.
My body, my life, my girls.
Maris, me.
Me.

STOLEN

Maris snaps awake
with a bone-rattling spasm, a sudden
alertness
and a gasping, grasping breath
desperate for the relief of
cold night air.

Around her the woods are quiet, still,
and there is a lightness
filtering through the trees
that suggests the storm is over, at last.
That is what Maris notices first.
Then, a second later, she sees herself
on the ground. The team surrounding her, and
her eyes open, her lips moving.

Oh, good, she thinks. *I'm not dead
after all.*

She tips her head to the side, curious.
Watching herself lying there, watching Nell
take her hand, watching August lay a jacket
over her shoulders. *Why are they
over there, when I'm
over here?*

And then:

*Why am I over there lying on the ground
when I'm standing right here?*

Then it slams into her.
The fall, Genevieve, the creature from her dreams
except they weren't dreams
and she saw its life
what it is, what it was, what it had done
what it planned to do
what it used her to do
used Genevieve, too
and there was the noise it made that
pulled Maris right out of her skin and—

It's hard to describe the feeling
of being in a body not your own.
Not human.
How your mind says *walk* but your feet no longer
work the same, your muscles
are not the muscles you pushed to their limit
in that sweaty school gym. It is a body
not yours
and it is a body that holds a lifetime of memories
that aren't yours
like a double exposure
two images layered one over the other

and you can't ignore them, can't
stop them seeping into your own mind, the faces you remember
and desire that consumed you, took you over
that you thought could never be satiated
until you found a girl

who finally saw you, who had everything you hungered for
so you took it, her, *me*

⤙⟷⤚

and I am trapped.

GONE

Maris screams—

and the sound that comes out of her
is not her own voice, not
her familiar poison-laced smooth voice but
something altogether inhuman, animal.

Maris screams, but it is as if
no one but her
can hear it
because none of the girls look up, none of them react at all. Only
continue tending
to the version of Maris on the ground, the one inhabited
by some being that is not herself, a driver
in a stolen car.

Maris screams and feels
the air whistling through the side of her skull
the working of her now-rotten jaw
the crumbling vessel that she has been forced into, tricked
inside.

Maris screams
a plea to anybody, anything listening, to
help *help please*
wake me up
break me out of this body
please—

≺≺∙≻≻

The sun breaks through the clouds
and Maris tips her new head back
stares through her new eyes at the sky above.
As if anyone will help her. As if
there is any help to be given, as if
she doesn't know already—memory soaked into
her new flesh—what she is, what she has become, what she will now
forever be.

Trapped inside the body of a monster.

⤙⤚

All that time I spent figuring out
how to get rid of fucking Genevieve
and all along somebody—
something—else
was figuring out how to get rid
of me

All that time thinking I was nothing
when I had no idea
how much less I could be

⤙⤚

Maris lets the last scream go
stands there, teeth bared
sun flashing over her slick black coat
as she watches the girls
ferrying their queen away
leaving her behind,
alone and waiting
for the woods to swallow her whole.

86

NELL

Nell's waiting on the hood of Maris's car.

Waiting for Maris after practice
is the kind of thing she used to do,
last fall, before all the shit that happened.
Before Nell knew what
a dead body looked like.

But it's not last fall.
That was more than a year ago
and it's winter
senior year
and things are different now.

The doors open
and out they spill, the girls
looking their post-practice best
hair wet from the showers
makeup rushed back onto faces, and this heat
that they radiate.

⤜⬌⤐

Maris leads the pack
like she always does
and Nell can't help it, can't help
staring at her. She looks better
than she ever has, all strong and
skin glowing, and
thrilled to be back in the gym, the place
that makes her happier than anything.

At least, Nell assumes that's still
how it is. She can't know for sure. Knowing
would mean talking to Maris
and she hasn't done that
since Maris came back to school last April
two months after that day and night in the woods,
showing off an impressive scar
that curls
around her left ankle
and crawls
up the inside of her leg,
enjoying everyone's eyes on her.

Nell tries not to think about that day too much, how
before first period she had kissed Maris in the parking lot
probably right in this exact spot,
and then how by last-period French
they were over, Maris ending things
in a single, blunt text.
She tries not to think about how her first thought had been
August, that
some part of her was sure
she played a part in this breakup somehow, despite
how Maris had always insisted she didn't
think of August
like that
how she always rolled her eyes
when Nell brought August up,
pointed out her
jealousy.

She tries not to think about how
she'd decided not to talk to Maris
ever again

the only appropriate response to someone
ending a relationship
over fucking *text*
but how her resolve had only lasted a week
and then she'd cornered Maris in the cafeteria
intending to tell her how cruel she'd been, how
pathetic
but what actually came out was "Is it
August? What, are you
in love with her
now?"
And Maris had rolled her eyes
like always
and walked away
not exactly denying it
not exactly saying no.

⊰⊹⊱

Nell shifts on the hood, an
icy breeze
seeping through the rips in her jeans. It had never been easy
her and Maris
but she'd loved her as much
as Maris would let her
gotten as close as she could
even while Maris pushed her away, always so willing
to give her everything to the team, to her friends,
but never to Nell.
Always choosing them
over her.
Always quick to laugh, or
cut
Nell down
with a bitchy barb

when Nell tried to talk about the future,
their future.
Nell had loved her
anyway
and that's why
she's sitting here waiting.
Probably
she should let all this go, let
Maris go, but—
Nell always ties up her loose ends, always does
her extra credit. Always was the difference
between her and Maris, wasn't it.

87

NELL

First there was the immediate after—
waiting for help to arrive. When it did
Nell watched them strap Maris to a board
and carry her out of the woods
to safety.
Led them
back through the trees
to where Genevieve's body lay.
The paramedics
told them all not to look
but it wasn't like Nell hadn't seen her already. It wasn't like
the image of her
black and blue and bloodied
rain-bloated skin
wasn't seared into her mind.

They emerged from the woods
into clear blue sky
storm vanished and bright citrine sun beaming
and there, where the woods gave way to civilization, was
Coach. Beside her a woman down on her knees
weeping
and Nell knew that must be Genevieve's mother.

And behind them, a small gathered crowd
watching, waiting to see
how the tragedy had unfolded
and Nell had stared at them
until her eyes blurred
and when she blinked and blinked
and looked again with clear eyes

she'd noticed her.
Maris's mom
hovering at the very edge of the crowd
hands plucking nervously at the collar of her coat but
no other movement—no
pushing through the bodies to reach her daughter, no
calling out *that's my girl, that's my baby*
only
waiting on the fringes
as if she were just another bystander gawking
as if it had taken everything in her
just to get that far
and now she wasn't sure
what to do.

Nell had wanted to go over
but then the ambulance's siren
had begun to wail
and it startled Nell
and when she looked back
Maris's mom was gone.

⤝⤞

Then there were the months after—

The story.
Two girls go into the woods
and only one comes out.

Of course it was a story
and Nell watched it swell—
at school and online, on the local news, even
for a quick moment
national.

But then a football player
murdered two sorority girls
a few hours away
and most everyone became more interested in that.
The reporters who did stick around
stubborn
only got one story out of Maris:
that she and Genevieve
had had their issues, sure, but
they'd faced their punishment for that
and they'd only gone into the woods
to figure out how to
coexist.
That Genevieve's death was
nothing
but a terrible accident, an
unforeseen storm.
"Or what," Maris is quoted
in one story as saying,
"do people think I brought that tree down
all by myself?
And then, what, threw
myself into the ravine
as a cover?
Sure.
That makes sense."
(There the reporter noted
that Maris had been deadpan,
droll,
but that her eyes had shone
with tears.)

⋖⟷⋗

Two girls went into the woods
and got caught in a storm.
One made it through
and one didn't.
That was the only real story there was.

⸻

That was the story, sure.
But Nell didn't dare ask Maris
whether it was also
the truth.
She was too afraid to know
the answer to the question
thrumming through her:

What the fuck
were you really *doing out there, with*
her,
Maris?

88

NELL

Now it's senior year
everything started over again
and those months in a hospital bed
—broken ribs, ankle surgery, a punctured lung,
and hypothermia—
are long over, Maris recovered and
fighting fit
so eager to show it off.

"Hey," Nell calls out
from her spot on the hood of Maris's car,
and the girls slow as one, staring.
After a moment Maris peels away from the pack
and the girls scatter as she walks away, like
without their leader
they don't know what to do with themselves.

"Hi," Maris says
when she's close but not too close, still
keeping a little distance
her only defense
since Nell has already invaded her space.
Maris shifts the strap of her gym bag higher
on her shoulder, and gives Nell
something close—but not too close—
to a smile. "Haven't done this in a while."

⊰⊹⊱

Nell slides off the hood
and shoves her hands in the pockets of her
ancient denim jacket, the one with the

white shearling collar
stained red in one particular spot
where Maris smeared her lipstick once.
"I wanted to tell you," Nell says, "I got into Bennington."
The email on her phone, the Congratulations!
We are pleased to welcome you
had arrived that morning, Nell opening it
heart in her throat. Early decision, her
only choice, and all the work
paid off, and when her parents were celebrating, the
only person Nell wanted to talk to
was Maris.

⊰⊹⊱

There's silence for a moment,
the distant screaming
of little kids on a playground.
"Bennington?" Maris looks blank, like she has
no fucking clue
what Nell is talking about, so Nell says, "Bennington?
College? I got in."

"You got in?" Something clicks, and Maris whirls
into motion, putting her cold hands
on either side of Nell's face and pressing
her lips to Nell's
hot and hard, punctuation at the end
of a story.
"Shit. Congratulations, genius bitch."

⊰⊹⊱

Nell put her fingers
to her lips
where Maris just kissed her.

That's
what she gets? A kiss?
After months of nothing
and after all the conflict college caused
between them
Maris's response to this news
is to kiss Nell
like that's something they still do, like
she thinks that's what Nell
wants?

(What *did* Nell want her to do?
Throw her arms around her?
No.
Scream
with delight?
No.
Nod slowly and say *I always knew you could do it*
while looking a little sad?
Yeah, maybe that.)

"Thanks." Nell
wipes her fingers on her jeans and tries to ignore
how that kiss felt wrong.
Not only because they don't do that anymore
but because—
it's hard to know, exactly. A different
taste, a different
energy. The feel of Maris's mouth
has left Nell
uneasy.

But Maris doesn't seem to notice
Nell's reaction, doesn't seem

to care at all, pulling her car keys
from her bag
halfway out of this moment already.
"I gotta go," Maris says. "But—good for
you. Cool shit and all that. Won't be
seeing you around that much longer, then,
right?"

⧏⧐

Maris is almost at the car door
when Nell grabs her arm
keeping her anchored. "I can't
do this anymore," Nell says, and Maris
looks at Nell's hand on her arm
and then up at Nell
with a disbelieving smile
almost like she's impressed. "Do what?"
Maris asks. "Bother me?"

That's better.
A little more like
the Maris who Nell used to know. "No,"
Nell says. "Pretend like
absolutely nothing's wrong. Like nothing happened
when you went into those woods."

"Who's pretending?"
Maris yanks her arm free of Nell's grip. "I have
the scars to remind me. There's a fucking
headstone to remind everyone else. I don't know
what more you want from me—"

"I wanna know the truth," Nell says, the words
hot. "Not the same story

you spun everyone else. *Why*
were you and Genevieve together that day? Why
did you take her into the woods?"

⊰⊱

Coach, the team, the cops—
they all seemed to buy Maris's story
wholesale
but they weren't the ones listening to Maris
talk constantly about taking Genevieve down.
They weren't the ones
who Maris asked for help, to find any dirt
that could be dug up on that girl.
They weren't the ones
who used to look right through Maris's
bitch act and see the desperation
simmering right beneath the surface. So excuse Nell
for not blindly believing
that all Maris wanted that day
was to kiss and make up with Genevieve.

⊰⊱

Maris gives one breath of
laughter. "Nell. Are you
accusing me of something?"
She tips her head to the side
so curious. "What, did you think
I took her out there
with something else in mind? Had a whole
plan or whatever, to
push her off the ridge
or something? Jesus Christ, Nell. I thought
you knew me better than that."

"I don't fucking know," Nell says. "All I know
is I don't believe
you would ever have willingly spent time alone
with Genevieve
unless you knew you were getting something you wanted
out of it.
And I know that
you came out of there
different, and no one but me
seems to see it, and no one but me
seems to care at all."

❮❮❯❯

"Different?"
The smile on Maris's face is shimmery,
there and then gone. "Hmm. Here's what it was, Nell. I finally did
what *you* kept telling me to do. I realized
the team couldn't go back to what it was
unless Genevieve and I could learn
to work together. I wanted
to settle shit. So did she.
So we go out there
and then the storm comes. I watch her get crushed
half to death
when the lightning rips that tree apart
and then I go looking for help
only to fall into the ravine. And I'm alone
for that whole night
waiting for it to end, thinking
that I'm about to die.
But then I don't.
But then she does.
And I have to go back to my life
knowing it was my fault

because I took her out there
and she'd still be here if it wasn't for
me. If I hadn't done
what *you* told me to.
So forgive me, Nell,
for acting *different*. For cutting my losses
with you. I mean,
that's what this is really about,
isn't it? I left you
before you could leave me, and that
was not the way you ever planned for it to go.
So fine, whatever.
I'm *different* now.
Believe what you want, Nell.
But don't waste my time with this shit
ever again."

⊰⊱

Nell watches Maris
get in her car, rev the engine, peel
out of the lot
and away from her.

She feels as if
she can see Maris's words left behind,
shimmering like that smile
in the air.

Fine, whatever.
I'm different *now.*

And she swallows her own words
that she never got the chance to say.

I really loved you, Maris.

Nell pulls her collar
close around her neck, eyes
on Maris in the distance.

"Six months,"
she says to herself. "Only
six months, and then I'm out
of this shithole town."

As if that will change things.
As if
that will make her forget
Maris—

whoever she is now.

89
NELL

Nell used to be
a sound sleeper. Now she thrashes
regular nightmares
of being out in the woods,
finding Genevieve, finding
Maris. Sometimes it plays out
just as it happened in reality.
Sometimes, like tonight,
they are psychedelic kaleidoscope
dreams.

Tonight she walks through the woods
in rain-soaked shorts and camisole
tonight she calls out, "Hello? Maris?"
and her voice comes back to her in chorus
birds crowing back *hello? hello? hello?*
Maris? Maris? Maris?

and Maris is there
running through the woods ahead
so tonight Nell chases after her
but she can never reach her, Maris
always just out of her grasp—

⟢⟡⟣

She wakes with a gasp
in sweat-soaked sheets.
Kicks them off,
sits up, says *"Fuck"*
into the dark as she rubs her eyes
until they sting, stream.

Down to the kitchen
where she swallows ice-cold water
standing in the open back door, sweat
chill on her skin now
as she looks out on the garden.

Nell turns to go inside, is
about to close the door
when there's movement
in her peripheral vision.

She whips around
catching only the quickest impression
of an animal, long legs, dark
and shining under the moon
vanishing into the trees
of next door's yard.
Stares for a minute, maybe two, maybe
more.
Nothing.

⬂⬀

Upstairs she climbs back into bed
and falls back to sleep, and in the morning
she barely remembers what she
saw. She barely remembers
the deer, vanishing.

90

TEAM

We love the sound of cheer,
still.
Palms slapping thighs harder, bodies smacking the mat, bones
creaking snapping clicking
but alive.
We feel that, all the time now,
how alive we are
when we are running circuits and
perfecting pyramids and
drilling choreo to a sweaty immaculate end.

Yes, lift, hit it, Coach yells.
We are more focused than ever
aware of what we could have lost
aware of who *was* lost.
And if we ever forget
we only need to look at Maris to remember.
She was the one out there
all night long in that storm
and look how she survived.
Recovered, rebuilt,
made it so we could return to our beloved home
and finds new limits to push against.

Sometimes we wonder
in the quiet moments
when we are alone
how it is that we knew
where to find Maris that night

but if we think too much
it feels
dangerous

and we decided long ago
that it was only
an odd coincidence
a trick of fate
like the stories people tell
of choosing to take a different route to work for the very first time
the one day there is a five-car pileup
or blowing off a date because something felt
off
only to later learn the date had been a
serial rapist.

Something like that,
we decided.

Besides
what other explanation
could there be?

—‹‹›—

Coach looks on, her smile slight,
the way it always is when she smiles at us now.
Remembering
who's missing.
But yet she smiles
and we still take that
as a sign of her pride
as we tumble in perfect sync

the pounding of our hands and feet
a clean drumline.

Lock our hands together
a basket for Maris to step into
and we lift her high high high.

91
DOE

Maris soars, arms
outstretched, toes
pointed, hips
lifted

suspended in the air
in time.

It feels so good
to work this hard.
To have a body at all,
to experience everything she craved
back when she was a creature with no home:

First the spring
healing, a tough pain
but a necessary one.

And then a summer spent
in constant motion
surrounded by her girls
driving too fast and
running everywhere
being seen
really seen
being touched, always touched
holding hands as they jumped into the reservoir
screaming as they hit the water.

Her body, steeped
in memory

in a way she hadn't anticipated
in a way that fills her again
with awe
with a wonder at what she has made possible.
As if the old Maris's spirit, soul
(*whatever it is you want to call all the ineffable things that make you
you,*
as the new Maris thinks of it)
had seeped into the bones, into the
marrow
left a muscle memory for the new Maris to take
and make her own.
Filling her with essential knowledge: how to
flip and jump and twist, how to
slick on inky eyeliner and scarlet lipstick, how to
slip in and out of the house that is now her home
without waking the woman who is now her mother
who doesn't seem to notice her daughter has
changed
exactly the way
Maris wants it.

I have a mother now,
Maris finds herself thinking often. *I am
somebody's daughter.*

No longer just a monster or a
god, but the
truest amalgamation of the two:
a girl.
She *is* Maris Larsen now,
with all it brings.

Except Nell, of course.

Couldn't keep her around
not with her perceptiveness
and love, *real* love,
a love that Maris could never truly see
but old Doe could see, did see, and
knew
she couldn't ever fully become Maris
if Nell kept too close.
She is the kind of girl
who asks questions
the kind of girl
who pushes and pries
and the new Maris did not do all that work
to have it undone
by a girl too curious for her own good.

Besides
she really has no interest in Nell
not when the team is there
not when sweet, sycophantic August
is there.

So maybe Nell had been right
that day in the cafeteria
eyes bright and cheeks flushed
as she asked
Is it August?
but nothing had happened then
and nothing has happened yet.
Maris knows, though,
that it will happen, she
and August,
and August will be so happy
to finally be with the girl she wants

that she won't question anything, won't want to
rock the boat,
and Maris will know what it's like
to answer to the new kind of desire
that simmers just below her surface
every second of every day.

And in the future
if she ever doubts
that leaving Nell was the right choice
Maris can think of Nell
jabbing at her in the parking lot the other day
still thinking
she knows everything and Maris is
some stupid bitch.
"Fine, whatever. I'm
different *now."*
She'd said it
and driven away
and laughed at Nell's ashen face
in the rearview.
She'd said *different*
but meant
better
and Nell would never understand that.

But it's okay
because she has the girls, the
team,
August and Prairie
and even little Lo
given a second chance
(or maybe just brought back
to fill a dead girl's shoes)

and the others
who adore her, purely
adore her.
Who love her even more now
if it's possible.
Now that they came close
to losing her.

⟶

Maris floats
at the top of the moment,
breathing in deep–

before snapping everything in,
twisting
spiraling down
to be caught in the arms
of her girls.

"Good!"
Coach calls out over the music. "Much
cleaner. Keep moving!"
Maris flashes her teeth
in a euphoric smile as she
bounces one foot onto the mat
and back up into Prairie's and August's hands.
She can't help those smiles,
how Coach's words of praise
feel when they hit.
"Down-up, one, good!"

In the air Maris extends
one leg behind her head, flooded
with amazement again

at what her body can do
at how *alive* she feels
at every moment.

She grips her leg
tight with one hand, the other
pointing out at an
imaginary watcher.
She doesn't fear falling
feels the girls' tight grip
around her ankle.
They would catch her
if she dropped.
They would throw themselves
beneath her, to make sure
she doesn't hit the ground.

Maris holds the pose, her muscles
screaming as they stretch, sweat
inching down her forehead, darkening
her sports bra.
Beneath it all there is the hum
the ever-present thrum of power.
It gets louder every day
the itch in her stronger every day
the desire to show the girls—the world—
what she is truly capable of.

Hush, hush.
Not now, not
yet. That time is coming
but in this moment,
she simply lets the power fill her.
Luxuriates in the freedom,

the *excitement*
of the destruction devastation delight
awaiting her.

With these girls
so much is possible,
Maris thinks
and she slicks her tongue
across her lips, the taste of her own sweat
exhilarating.
I can't wait to see
the chaos
we can create.

92
TEAM

Now we hold Maris high
bearing her weight
all our focus on her.
We almost lost her
and it is wrong to say we are
glad Genevieve is dead instead of her
but we think it anyway, often.
We have our leader back and we
are going to follow her wherever she might take us.
We are each other's family. Us, who want each other
when nobody else does
who hear each other
when nobody wants to listen. Maris
she listens, she holds us, she sees.

So we are hers
and she is ours
till death
or the end of the world.

ACKNOWLEDGMENTS

My heartfelt thanks to the following:

My powerhouse editor Stacey Barney and every single person at Nancy Paulsen Books and across Penguin Young Readers Group for all their hard work on this book.

My incredible agent Faye Bender who saw the magic in this book and made it happen.

Rory Power, who made me believe in this book when I needed it most.

Maggie Horne, who believed in it when it was just fragments in her inbox.

Janet McNally, my #1 podcaster.

Diana Hurlburt, who always has the perfect bloom to bring joy.

My family for their constant support.